The
Wishing-Chair
Again

Enjoy these other books by

Enid Blyton

Enid Blyton

The
Wishing-Chair
Again

HODDER

HODDER CHILDREN'S BOOKS
The Wishing Chair Again first published in Great Britain in 1950
by George Newnes
This edition first published in 2018 by Egmont UK Limited
This edition published in 2020 by Hodder & Stoughton Limited

1 3 5 7 9 10 8 6 4 2

Enid Blyton ® and Enid Blyton's signature are registered trade marks of
Hodder & Stoughton Limited
Text © 2020 Hodder & Stoughton Limited
Cover illustration by Mark Beech and interior illustrations by Rene Cloke.
Illustrations © 2020 Hodder & Stoughton Limited

A CIP catalogue record for this book is available from the British Library.

ISBN 978 1 444 95949 9

Printed and bound in Great Britain by Clays Ltd, Elcograf S.p.A

The paper and board used in this book are made from wood from responsible sources.

CONTENTS

CHAPTER 1
HOME FOR THE HOLIDAYS

Mollie and Peter had just arrived home for the holidays. Their schools had broken up the same day, which was very lucky, and Mother had met them at the station.

They hugged her hard. 'Mother! It's grand to see you again. How's everyone?'

'Fine,' said Mother. 'The garden's looking lovely, your bedrooms are all ready for you, and your playroom at the bottom of the garden is longing for you to go there and play as usual.'

The two children looked at one another. They had a big Secret. One they couldn't possibly mention even in their letters to one another at school. How they were longing to talk about it now!

'Can we just pop down to our playroom first of all?' asked Peter when they got home.

'Oh, no, dear!' said Mother. 'You must come upstairs and wash – and help me to unpack your things. You will have plenty of time to spend in your playroom these holidays.'

The children's Secret was in their playroom – and they so badly wanted to see it again. They went upstairs and washed and then went down to tea.

'Can we go to our playroom after we've helped you to unpack?' asked Peter.

Mother laughed. 'Very well – leave me to unpack, and go along. I expect you want to see if I've given away any of your things. Well, I haven't. I never do that without asking you.'

After tea Peter spoke to Mollie in a low voice.

'Mollie! Do you think Binky will be down in our playroom waiting for us – with the Wishing-Chair?'

'I do hope so,' said Mollie. 'Oh, Peter, it was dreadful trying to keep our Secret all the term long and never saying anything to anyone.'

'Well, it's such a marvellous Secret it's worth keeping well,' said Peter. 'Do you remember when we first got the Wishing-Chair, Mollie?'

'Yes,' said Mollie. 'We went to a funny little shop that sold old, old things to get something for Mother's birthday, and we saw heaps of strange enchanted things there. And we were frightened and huddled together in an old chair . . .'

'And we wished we were safe back at home,' said Peter, 'and, hey presto! the chair grew little red wings on its legs, and flew out of a window with us, and took us back to our playroom!'

'Yes. And it wouldn't go back to the shop even when we commanded it to,' said Mollie. 'So we had to keep it – our very own Wishing-Chair.'

'And do you remember how we went off in it again, and came to a castle where there was a giant who kept a little servant called Binky?' said Peter. 'And we rescued him and took him home in the Wishing-Chair with us.'

'That was lovely,' said Mollie. 'And after that Binky lived down in our playroom and looked after the chair for us . . .'

'And told us when it grew its wings so that we could all fly off in it again and have wonderful adventures,' said Peter. 'Then we had to go to school and leave it.'

'But it didn't matter really, because Binky took the chair home to his mother's cottage and lived with her and took care of it for us,' said Mollie.

'And he said he'd come back as soon as we came home for the holidays, and bring the chair with him so that we could go adventuring again,' finished Peter. 'If Mother only knew that's the reason we want to get down to the playroom – to see if Binky is there, and to see the dear old Wishing-Chair again.'

Peter found the key. 'Come on, Mollie – let's go and see all our toys again.'

'And the Wishing-Chair,' said Mollie in a whisper. '*And* Binky.'

They rushed downstairs and out into the garden. It was the end of July and the garden was full of flowers; it was lovely to be home! No more lessons for eight weeks, no more preps.

They raced down to the playroom, which was really a big, airy shed at the bottom of the garden. Peter slid the key into the lock. 'Binky!' he called. 'Are you here?'

He unlocked the door. The children went into the playroom and looked round. It was a nice room, with a big rug on the floor, shelves for their books and toys, a

3

cot with Mollie's old dolls in it, and a large doll's house in the corner.

But there was no Wishing-Chair and no Binky the pixie! The children stared round in dismay.

'He's not here,' said Peter. 'He said he would come today with the chair. I gave him the date and he wrote it down in his notebook.'

'I hope he's not ill,' said Mollie. They looked all round the playroom, set the musical box going and opened the windows.

They felt disappointed. They had so looked forward to seeing Binky, and to sitting once more in the Wishing-Chair. Suddenly a little face looked in at the door.

Mollie gave a shout. 'Binky!' It's you! We were so worried about you! We hoped you'd be here.'

Both children gave the little pixie a hug. Binky grinned. 'Well, how could I be here waiting for you if the door was locked and the windows fastened, silly? I may be a pixie, but I can't fly through locked doors. I *have* missed you. Were you very bored away at school?'

'Oh, *no*,' said Peter. 'Boarding school is simply lovely. We both loved it – but we're jolly glad to be home again.'

'Binky, where's the Wishing-Chair?' asked Mollie anxiously. 'Nothing's happened to it, has it? Have you got it with you?'

'Well, I brought it here this morning,' said Binky, 'but when I found the door of the playroom was locked and couldn't get in I hid it under the hedge at the bottom of the garden. But you'd be surprised how many people nearly found it!'

'But nobody goes to the bottom of the garden!' said Peter.

'Oh, don't they!' said Binky. 'Well, first of all your gardener thought he'd cut the hedge there today, and I had an awful job dragging the chair from one hiding place to another. Then an old woman came by, and she almost saw it, but I barked like a dog and she ran away.'

The children laughed. 'Poor old Binky! You must have been glad when we got here at last.'

'Let's go and get it,' said Peter. 'I'm hoping to sit in it again. Has it grown its wings much since we left it with you, Binky?'

'Not once,' said Binky. 'Funny, isn't it? It's just stood in my mother's kitchen like any ordinary chair, and never grown even one red wing! I think it was waiting for you to come back.'

'I hope it was – because then it may grow its wings heaps of times,' said Peter, 'and we'll go off on lots of adventures.'

They went to the hedge. 'There it is!' said Mollie in excitement. 'I can see one of its legs sticking out.'

They dragged out the old chair. 'Just the same!' said Peter in delight. 'And how well you've kept it, Binky. It's polished so brightly.'

'Ah, that was my mother did that,' said Binky. 'She said such a wonderful chair should have a wonderful polish, and she was at it every day, rub, rub, rub till the chair groaned!'

Peter carried the chair back to the playroom. Binky went in front to make sure there was nobody looking. They didn't want any questions asked about why chairs should be hidden in hedges. They set it down in its old place in the playroom. Then they all climbed into it.

'It's just the same,' said Peter. 'We feel a bit more squashed than usual because Mollie and I seem to have grown at school. But you haven't grown, Binky.'

'No. I shan't grow any more,' said Binky. 'Don't you wish the chair would grow its wings and go flapping off somewhere with us now?'

'Oh, *yes*,' said Mollie. 'Chair, do grow your wings – just to please us! Even if it's only to take us a little way up into the air and back.'

But the chair didn't. The children looked anxiously down at its legs to see if the red buds were forming that sprouted into wings, but there was nothing there.

'It's no good,' said Binky. 'It won't grow its wings just because it's asked. It can be very obstinate, you know. All I hope is that it hasn't forgotten *how* to grow wings after being still so long. I shouldn't like the magic to fade away.'

This was a dreadful thought. The children patted the arms of the chair. 'Dear Wishing-Chair! You haven't forgotten how to grow wings, have you?'

The chair gave a remarkable creak, a very long one. Everyone laughed. 'It's all right!' said Binky. 'That's its way of telling us it hasn't forgotten. A creak is the only voice it's got!'

Mother came down the garden. 'Children! Daddy's home. He wants to see you!'

'Right!' called back Peter. He turned to Binky. 'See you tomorrow, Binky. You can cuddle up on the old sofa as usual, with the rug and the cushion, for the night. You'll live in our playroom, won't you, as you did before, and tell us when the chair grows its wings?'

'Yes. I shall like to live here once more,' said Binky.

The children ran back to the house. They had a very nice evening indeed telling their parents everything that had happened in the term. Then off they went to bed, glad to be in their own dear little rooms again.

But they hadn't been asleep very long before Peter began to dream that he was a rat being shaken by a dog. It was a very unpleasant dream, and he woke up with a jump.

It was Binky shaking him by the arm. 'Wake up!' whispered the pixie. 'The chair's grown its wings already. They're big, strong ones, and they're flapping like anything. If you want an adventure, hurry up!'

Well! What a thrill! Peter woke Mollie and they pulled on their clothes very quickly and ran down the garden. They heard a loud flapping noise as they reached the playroom shed. 'It's the chair's wings,' panted Binky. 'Come on – we'll just sit in it before it goes flying off!'

CHAPTER 2
OFF ON AN ADVENTURE

The children raced in at the playroom door and made for the Wishing-Chair. They could see it easily in the bright moonlight. It was just about to fly off when they flung themselves in it. Binky squeezed between them, sitting on the top of the back of the chair.

'Good old Wishing-Chair!' said Peter. 'You didn't take long to grow your wings! Where are we going?'

'Where would you like to go?' said Binky. 'Wish, and we'll go wherever you wish.'

'Well – let me see – oh dear, I simply can't think of anywhere,' said Mollie. 'Peter, you wish – quickly.'

'Er – Wishing-Chair, take us to – to – oh, goodness knows where I want it to go!' cried Peter. 'I simply don't . . .'

But dear me, the Wishing-Chair was off! It flapped its wings very strongly indeed, rose up into the air, flew towards the door and out of it – then up into the air it went, flapping its red wings in the moonlight.

Binky giggled. 'Oh, Peter – you said "Take us to Goodness Knows Where",' said the pixie. 'And that's just about where we're going!'

'Gracious! – is there *really* a land called Goodness

Knows Where?' said Peter, in surprise.

'Yes. Don't you remember when we went to the Land of Scallywags once, the Prince of Goodness Knows Where came to see me,' said Binky. 'I was pretending to be a King. Well, I suppose it's *his* Land we're going to.'

'Where is it?' said Mollie.

'Goodness knows!' said Binky. 'I don't. I've never met anyone who did, either.'

'The Wishing-Chair seems to know,' said Peter, as it flew higher and higher in the air.

But it didn't know, really. It dropped downwards after a time and came to a tiny village. Peter leaned out of the chair and gazed with great interest at it. 'Look at that bridge,' he said. 'Hey, Chair, whatever are you doing now?'

The chair hadn't landed in the village. It had flown a few feet above the strange little houses and had then shot upwards again.

The chair flew on again, and then came to a heaving mass of water. Was it the sea? Or a lake? The children didn't know. 'Look at that lovely silver moon-path on the sea,' said Mollie, leaning out of the chair. 'I'm sure it leads to the moon!'

The chair seemed to think so too. It flew down to the water, got on the moon-path and followed it steadily, up and up and up.

'Hey! This isn't the way to Goodness Knows Where!' said Binky, in alarm. 'It's the way to the moon. Don't be silly, Chair!'

The chair stopped and hovered in mid-air as if it had

heard Binky and was changing its mind. To the children's great relief it left the moon-path and flew on till it came to a little island. This was perfectly round and flat, and had one big tree standing up in the middle of it. Under the tree was a boat and someone was fast asleep in it.

'Oh, that's my cousin, Sleep-Alone,' said Binky, in surprise. 'He's a funny fellow, you know – can't bear to sleep if anyone else is within miles of him. So he has a boat and an aeroplane, and each night he takes one or the other and goes off to some lonely place to sleep. Hey there, Sleep-Alone!'

Binky's shout made the children jump. The chair jumped too, and Mollie was almost jerked off. She clutched at the arm.

The little man in the boat awoke. He was more like a brownie than a pixie and had a very long beard, which he had wound neatly round his neck like a scarf. He was most surprised to see the Wishing-Chair landing on the island just near him. He scowled at Binky.

'What's all this? Coming and shouting at me in the middle of the night! Can't I ever sleep alone?'

'You always do!' said Binky. 'Don't be so cross. Aren't you surprised to see us?'

'Not a bit,' said Sleep-Alone. 'You're always turning up when I don't want to have company. Go away. I've a cold coming on and I feel gloomy.'

'Is that why you've got your beard wound round your neck – to keep it warm?' asked Mollie. 'How long is it when it unwinds?'

'I've no idea,' said Sleep-Alone, who seemed a disagreeable fellow. 'Where are you going in the middle of the night? Are you quite mad?'

'We're going to Goodness Knows Where,' said Binky. 'But the chair doesn't seem to know the way. Do *you* know it?'

'Goodness knows where it is,' said Sleep-Alone, pulling his beard tighter round his neck. 'Better ask her.'

The children and Binky stared. 'Ask Who?' said Binky.

'Goodness, of course,' said Sleep-Alone, settling down in his boat again.

'Oh – is Goodness the name of a person then?' said Mollie, suddenly seeing light.

'You are a very stupid little girl, I think,' said Sleep-Alone. 'Am I to go on and on saying the same thing over and over again? Now goodnight, and go and find Goodness if you want to disturb someone else.'

'Where does she live?' bellowed Binky in Sleep-Alone's ear, afraid that he would go to sleep before he told them anything else.

That was too much for Sleep-Alone. He shot up and reached for an oar. Before Binky could get out of the way he had given him such a slap with the oar blade that Binky yelled at the top of his voice. Then Sleep-Alone turned on the two children, waving the oar in a most alarming manner.

Peter pulled Mollie to the chair. He put out a hand and dragged Binky to it too, shouting, 'Go to Goodness, Chair, go to Goodness, wherever she is!' Up rose the chair so very suddenly that Binky fell off and had to be dragged up again.

Sleep-Alone roared after them. 'Now I'm thoroughly awake and I shan't go to sleep tonight. You wait until I see you again, Binky, I'll fly you off in my aeroplane to the Land of Rubbish and drop you in the biggest dustbin there!'

'He's not a very nice cousin to have, is he?' said Mollie, when they had left Sleep-Alone well behind. 'I hope we don't see him again.'

'Who is this Goodness, I wonder?' said Peter.

'Never heard of her,' said Binky. 'But the chair really seems to know where it's going this time, so I suppose it knows Goodness all right!'

The Wishing-Chair was flying steadily to the east now. It had left the water behind and was now over some land that lay shining in the moonlight. The children could see towers and pinnacles, but they were too high up to see anything clearly.

The chair suddenly flew downwards. It came to a small cottage. All three of its chimneys were smoking. The smoke was green, and the children knew that was a sign that a witch lived there.

'I say – that's witch-smoke,' said Peter, nervously. He had met witches before on his adventures, and he knew quite a bit about them.

'I hope the chair has come to the right place,' said Mollie, as it landed gently on the path just outside the door of the little cottage.

They jumped off the chair, dragged it under a tree and went to knock at the door. A little old woman opened it. She looked so ordinary that the children felt sure she wasn't a witch.

'Please, is this where Goodness lives?' asked Binky, politely.

'Not exactly. But I keep a Book of Goodness,' said the old woman. 'Have you come to seek advice from it?'

'Well – we rather wanted to know where the Land of Goodness Knows Where is,' said Binky. 'And we were told that only Goodness knew where it was!'

'Ah, well – you will have to consult my Goodness Book then,' said the old woman. 'Wait till I get on my things.'

She left them in a tiny kitchen and disappeared. When she came back, what a difference in her! She had on a tall, pointed hat, the kind witches and wizards wear, and a great cloak that kept blowing out round her as if she kept a wind under its folds. She no longer looked an ordinary little old woman – she was a proper witch, but her eyes were kind and smiling.

She took down from a shelf a very big book indeed. It seemed to be full of names and very tiny writing. 'What are your names?' she asked. 'I must look you up in my Goodness Book before you can be told what you want to know.'

They told her, and she ran her finger down column after column. 'Ah – Peter – helped a boy with his homework for a whole week last term – remembered his mother's birthday – owned up when he did something wrong – my word, there's a whole list of goodness here. And Mollie too – gave up her half-holiday to stay in with a friend who was ill – told the truth when she knew she would get into trouble for doing so – quite a long list of goodness for her too.'

'Now me,' said Binky. 'I've been living with my mother. I do try to be good to her.' The old woman ran her finger down the list again and nodded her head. 'Yes – did his mother's shopping and never grumbled – took her breakfast in bed each day – never forgot to feed the dog – yes, you're all right, Binky.'

'What happens next?' said Peter. The witch took her Book of Goodness to a curious hole in the middle of the kitchen floor. It suddenly glowed as if it were full of shining water. The witch held the book over it, and out of it slid little gleaming streaks of colour. 'That's your Goodness going into the magic pool,' she said. 'Now, ask what you want to know.'

Binky asked, in rather a trembling voice, 'We want to know where the Land of Goodness Knows Where is.'

And dear me, a very extraordinary thing happened! On the top of the shining water appeared a shimmering map. In the middle of it was marked 'Land of Goodness Knows Where'. The children and Binky leaned over it eagerly, trying to see how to get there.

'Look – we fly due east to the rising sun,' began Binky; then he stopped. They had all heard a very peculiar noise outside. A loud creaking noise.

'The chair's calling to us!' cried Binky and he rushed to the door. 'Oh, look – it's flying away – and somebody else is in it. Somebody's stolen the Wishing-Chair! Whatever shall we do?'

CHAPTER 3

WHERE CAN THE WISHING-CHAIR BE?

'Who's taken our chair?' cried Peter, in despair. 'We can't get back home now. Come back, Chair!'

But the chair was under somebody else's command now, and it took no notice. It rose higher and higher and was soon no more than a speck in the moonlight. The three stared at one another, very upset indeed.

'Our very first adventure – and the chair's gone,' said Mollie, in a shaky voice. 'It's too bad. Right at the very beginning of the holidays too.'

'Who was that taking our chair – do you know?' Binky asked the witch, who was busy smoothing the surface of the water in the hole in the floor with what looked like a fine brush. The map that had shone there was now gone, and the water was empty of reflection or picture. The children wondered what would appear there next.

The witch shook her head. 'No – I don't know,' she said. 'I didn't hear anyone out there because I was so busy in here with you. All kinds of people come to ask me questions, you know, just as you did, and watch to see what appears in my magic pool. Some of the people are very odd. I expect it was one of them – and he saw your chair, knew what it was and flew off in it at once. It would be very valuable to him.'

'I do think it's bad luck,' said Mollie, tears coming into her eyes. 'Our very first night. And how are we to get back home again?'

'You can catch the Dawn Bus if you like,' said the witch. 'It will be along here in a few minutes' time. As soon as the sky turns silver in the east it comes rumbling along. Now, listen, I can hear the bus.'

Wondering whatever kind of people caught the Dawn Bus, Mollie and the others went out to catch it. It came rumbling along, looking more like a toy bus than a real one. It was crammed with little folk of all kinds! Brownies with long beards leaned against one another, fast asleep. Two tiny fairies slept with their arms round each other. A wizard nodded off to sleep, his pointed hat getting more and more crooked each moment – and three goblins yawned so widely that their mischievous little faces seemed all mouth!

'The bus is full,' said Mollie, in dismay.

'Sit in front with the driver, then,' said the witch. 'Go on, or you'll miss it!'

So Mollie, Peter and Binky squashed themselves in front with the driver. He was a brownie, and wore his beard tied round his waist and made into a bow behind. It looked very odd.

'Plenty of room,' he said, and moved up so far that he couldn't reach the wheel to drive the bus. 'You drive it,' he said to Binky, and, very pleased indeed, Binky took the wheel.

But, goodness gracious me, Binky was no good at

all at driving buses! He nearly hit a tree, swerved violently and went into an enormous puddle that splashed everyone from head to foot, and then went into a ditch and out of it at top speed.

By this time all the passengers were wide awake and shouting in alarm. 'Stop him! He's mad! Fetch a policeman!'

The bus-driver was upset to hear all the shouting. He moved back to his wheel so quickly that Binky was flung out into the road. He got up and ran after the bus, shouting.

But the bus-driver wouldn't stop. He drove on at top speed, though Mollie and Peter begged him to go back for Binky.

'I don't know how to back this bus,' said the brownie driver, solemnly. 'I keep meaning to learn but I never seem to have time. Most annoying. Still, I hardly ever want to back.'

'Well, *stop* if you don't know how to back,' cried Peter, but the brownie looked really horrified.

'What – stop before I come to a stopping-place? You must be mad. No, no – full speed ahead is my motto. I've got to get all these tired passengers back home as soon as possible.'

'Why are they so tired?' said Mollie, seeing the wizard beginning to nod again.

'Well, they've all been to a moonlight dance,' said the driver. 'Very nice dance too. I went to it. Last time I went to one I was so tired when I drove my bus home that I fell asleep when I was driving it. Found myself in the Land of Dreamland in no time, and used up every drop of my petrol.'

This all sounded rather extraordinary. Mollie and Peter looked at him nervously, hoping that he wouldn't fall asleep this time. Mollie could hardly keep her eyes open. She worried about Binky. Would he find his way back to the playroom all right? And, oh dear, what were they going to do about the Wishing-Chair?

Just as she was thinking that she fell sound asleep. Peter was already asleep. The driver looked at them, gave a grunt, and fell asleep himself.

So, of course, the bus went straight on to Dreamland again, and when Peter and Mollie awoke, they were not in the bus at all but in their own beds! Mollie tried to remember all that had happened. Was it real or was it a dream? She thought she had better go and ask Peter.

She went to his room. He was sitting up in bed and rubbing his eyes. 'I know what you've come to ask me,' he said. 'The same question I was coming to ask *you*. Did we dream it or didn't we? And how did we get back here?'

'That bus must have gone to the Land of Dreamland again,' said Mollie. 'But how we got here I don't know. I'm still in my day-clothes – look!'

'So am I,' said Peter, astonished. 'Well, that shows it was real then. Oh dear – do you suppose Binky is back yet?'

'Shall we go and see now?' said Mollie.

But the breakfast bell rang just then. They cleaned their teeth, did their hair, washed and tidied their crumpled clothes – then down they went.

After breakfast they ran down to the playroom at the

bottom of the garden.

Binky was there! He was lying on the sofa fast asleep.

'Binky, wake up!' shouted Mollie.

He didn't stir. Mollie shook him.

'Don't wake me, Mother,' murmured Binky, trying to turn over. 'Let me sleep.'

'Binky – you're not at home, you're here,' said Peter, shaking him again.

Binky rolled over on his other side – and fell right off the sofa!

That woke him up with a jerk. He gave a shout of alarm, opened his eyes and sat up.

'I say, did you tip me off the sofa?' he said. 'You needn't have done that.'

'We didn't. You rolled off yourself,' said Mollie with a laugh. 'How did you get back last night, Binky?'

'I walked all the way – so no wonder I'm tired this morning,' said Binky, his eyes beginning to close again. 'I did think you might have stopped the bus and picked me up.'

'The driver wouldn't stop,' explained Peter. 'He was awfully silly, really. We were very upset at leaving you behind.'

'The thing is, Binky – how are we going to find out where the Wishing-Chair has gone?' said Peter, seriously. 'It's only the beginning of the holidays, you know, and if we don't get it back the holidays will be very dull indeed.'

'I'm too sleepy to think,' said Binky, and fell asleep again. Mollie shook him impatiently.

'Binky, do wake up. We really are very worried about the Wishing-Chair.'

But there was no waking Binky this time! He was so sound asleep that he didn't even stir when Mollie tickled him under the arms.

The two children were disappointed. They stayed in the playroom till dinner-time, but Binky didn't wake up. They went indoors to have their dinner and then came down to see if Binky was awake yet. He wasn't!

Just then there came a soft tapping at the door and a little voice said: 'Binky! Are you there?'

Peter opened the door. Outside stood a small elf, looking rather alarmed. He held a leaflet in his hand.

'Oh, I'm very sorry,' he said. 'I didn't know you were here. I wanted Binky.'

'He's so fast asleep we can't wake him,' said Peter. 'Can we give him a message?'

'Yes. Tell him I saw this notice of his,' said the little elf, and showed it to the children. It was a little card, printed in Binky's writing:

> 'Lost or stolen. Genuine Wishing-Chair.
> Please give any information about it to
> BINKY.
> (I shall be in the playroom.)'

'Anything else?' asked Peter.

'Well – you might tell him I think I know where the chair is,' said the little elf, shyly.

'*Do* you?' cried both children. 'Well, tell us, then – it's our chair!'

'There's to be a sale of furniture at a brownie's shop

not far away,' said the elf, 'and there are six old chairs to be sold. Now, I know he only had five – so where did the sixth come from? Look, here's a picture of them.'

The children looked at the picture. Peter gave a cry. 'Why, they're *exactly* like our chair. Are they *all* wishing-chairs, then?'

'Oh, no. Your chair is very unusual. I expect what happened is that the thief who flew off on your chair wondered how to hide it. He remembered somebody who had five chairs just like it and offered it to him to make the set complete.'

'I don't see why he should do that,' said Mollie, puzzled.

'Wait,' said the elf. 'Nobody would suspect that one of the six chairs was a wishing-chair – and I've no doubt that the thief will send someone to bid a price for all six; and when he gets them he will suddenly say that he has discovered one of them is a wishing-chair, and sell it to a wizard for a sack of gold!'

'I think that's a horrid trick,' said Mollie, in disgust. 'Well, it looks as if we'll have to go along to this furniture shop and have a look at the chairs, to see if we can find out which one is ours. Oh dear, I do wish Binky would wake up.'

'You'd better go as soon as you can,' said the elf. 'The thief won't lose much time in buying it back, with the other chairs thrown in!'

So they tried to wake Binky again – but he just wouldn't wake up! 'We'll have to go by ourselves,' said Peter at last. 'Elf, will you show us the way? You will? Right, then off we go! Leave your message on the table for Binky to see, then he'll guess where we've gone!'

CHAPTER 4
HUNTING FOR THE CHAIR

The elf took them a very surprising way. He guided them to the bottom of the garden and through a gap in the hedge. Then he took them to the end of the field and showed them a dark ring of grass.

'We call that a fairy ring,' said Mollie. 'Sometimes it has little toadstools all the way round it.'

'Yes,' said the elf. 'Well, I'll show you a use for fairy rings. Sit down on the dark grass, please.'

Mollie and Peter sat down. They had to squeeze very close together indeed, because the ring of grass was not large. The elf felt about in it as if he was looking for something. He found it – and pressed hard!

And down shot the ring of grass as if it were a lift! The children, taken by surprise, gasped and held on to one another. They stopped with such a bump that they were shaken off the circle of grass and rolled away from it, over and over.

'So sorry,' said the elf. 'I'm afraid I pressed the button rather hard! Are you hurt?'

'No – not really,' said Mollie. As she spoke she saw the circle of grass shoot up again and fit itself neatly back into the field.

'Well – we do learn surprising things,' she said. 'What next, elf?'

'Along this passage,' said the elf, and trotted in front of them. It was quite light underground, though neither of the children could see where the lighting came from. They passed little, brightly painted doors on their way, and Peter longed to rat-tat at the knockers and see who answered.

They came to some steps and went up them, round and round in a spiral stairway. Wherever were they coming to? At the top was a door. The elf opened it – and there they were, in a small round room, very cosy indeed.

'What a strange, round room,' said Peter, surprised. 'Oh – I know why it's round. It's inside the trunk of a tree! I've been in a tree-house before!'

'Guessed right first time!' said the elf. 'This is where I live. I'd ask you to stop and have a cup of tea with me, but I think we'd better get on and see those chairs before anything happens to them.'

'Yes. So do I,' said Peter. 'Where's the door out of the tree?'

It was fitted in so cunningly that it was impossible to see it unless you knew where it was. The elf went to it at once, of course, and opened it. They all stepped out into a wood. The elf shut the door. The children looked back at it. No – they couldn't possibly, possibly tell where it was now – it was so much part of the tree!

'Come along,' said the elf and they followed him through the wood. They came to a lane and then to a very neat village, all the houses set in tiny rows, with a little square green in the middle, and four white ducks looking very clean on a round pond in the centre of the green.

'How very proper!' said Peter. 'Not a blade of grass out of place.'

'This is Pin Village,' said the elf. 'You've heard the saying, "As neat as a pin," I suppose? Well, this is Pin – always very neat and tidy and the people of the village, the Pins, never have a button missing or a hair blowing loose.'

The children saw that it was just as the elf said – the people were so tidy and neat that the children felt dirty and untidy at once. 'They all look a bit like pins dressed up and walking about,' said Mollie with a giggle. 'Well,

I'm glad I know what "neat as a pin" really means. Do they ever run, or make a noise, or laugh?'

'Sh! Don't laugh at them,' said the elf. 'Now look – do you see that shop at the corner? It isn't kept by a Pin; it's kept by Mr Polish. He sells furniture.'

'And he's called Polish because he's always polishing it, I suppose,' said Mollie with a laugh.

'Don't be too clever!' said the elf. 'He doesn't do any polishing at all – his daughter Polly does that.'

'Here's the shop,' said Mollie, and they stood and looked at it. She nudged Peter. 'Look,' she whispered, 'six chairs – all exactly alike. How are we to tell which is ours?'

'Come and have a look,' said Peter, and they went inside with the elf. A brownie girl was busy polishing away at the chairs, making them shine and gleam.

'There's Polly Polish,' said Mollie to Peter. She must have heard what they said and looked up. She smiled. She was a nice little thing, with pointed ears like Binky, and very green eyes.

'Hallo,' she said.

Mollie smiled back. 'These are nice chairs, aren't they?' she said. 'You've got a whole set of them!'

'Yes – my father, Mr Polish, was very pleased,' said Polly. 'He's only had five for a long time, and people want to buy chairs in sixes, you know.'

'How did he manage to get the sixth one?' asked Peter.

'It was a great bit of luck,' said Polly. 'There's a goblin called Tricky who came along and said he wanted to sell an old chair that had once belonged to his grandmother – and when he showed it to us, lo and behold, it was the missing sixth chair of our set! So we bought it from him, and there it is. I expect now we shall be able to sell the whole set. Someone is sure to come along and buy it.'

'Which chair did the goblin bring you?' asked Peter, looking hard at them all.

'I don't know now,' said Polly, putting more polish on her duster and rubbing very hard at a chair. 'I've been cleaning them and moving them about, you know – and they're all mixed up.'

The children stared at them in despair. They all looked exactly alike to them! Oh dear – how could they possibly tell which was their chair?

Then Polly said something very helpful, though she didn't know it! 'You know,' she said, 'there's something strange about one of these chairs. I've polished and polished the back of it, but it seems to have a little hole there, or something. Anyway, I can't make that little bit come bright and shining.'

The children pricked up their ears at once. 'Which chair?' said Peter. Polly showed them the one. It certainly seemed as if it had a hole in the back of it. Peter put his finger there – but the hole wasn't a hole! He could feel quite solid wood there!

And then he knew it was their own chair. He whispered to Mollie.

'Do you remember last year, when somebody made our Wishing-Chair invisible? And we had to get some paint to make it visible again?'

'Oh, yes!' whispered back Mollie. 'I do remember – and we hadn't enough paint to make one little bit at the back of the chair become visible again, so it always looked as if there was a hole there, though there wasn't really!'

'Yes – and that's the place that poor Polly has been polishing and polishing,' said Peter. 'Well – now we know that this is our chair all right! If only it would grow its wings we could sit on it straight away and wish ourselves home again!' He ran his fingers down the legs of the chair to see if by any chance there were some bumps growing, that would mean wings were coming once more. But there weren't.

'Perhaps the wings will grow again this evening,' said Mollie. 'Let's go and have tea with the elf in his tree-house and then come back here again and see if the chair has grown its wings.'

The elf was very pleased to think they would come back to tea with him. Before they went Peter looked hard at the chairs. 'You know,' he said to Mollie, 'I think we'd better just tie a ribbon round our own chair, so that if by any chance we decided to take it and go home with it quickly before anyone could stop us, we'd know immediately which it was.'

'That's a good idea,' said Mollie. She had no hair-ribbon, so she took her little blue handkerchief and knotted it round the right arm of the chair.

'What are you doing that for?' asked Polly Polish in surprise.

'We'll tell you some other time, Polly,' said Mollie.

'Don't untie it, will you? It's to remind us of something. We'll come back again after tea.'

They went off with the elf. He asked them to see if they could find his door-handle and turn it to get into his tree-house – but, however much they looked and felt about, neither of them could make out where the closely-fitting door was! It's no wonder nobody ever knows which the tree-houses are!

The elf had to open the door for them himself, and in they went. He got them a lovely tea, with pink jellies that shone like a sunset, and blancmange that he had made in the shape of a little castle.

'I do wonder if Binky's woken up yet,' said Mollie, at last. 'No, thank you, elf, I can't possibly eat any more. It was a really lovely tea.'

'Now what about going back to the shop and seeing if we can't take our chair away?' said Peter. 'We'll send Binky to explain about it later – the thing is, we really must take it quickly, or that goblin called Tricky will send someone to buy all the set – and our chair with it!'

So off they went to the shop – and will you believe it, there were no chairs there! They were all gone from the window! The children stared in dismay.

They went into the shop. 'What's happened to the chairs?' they asked Polly.

'Oh, we had such a bit of luck just after you had gone,' said Polly. 'Somebody came by, noticed the chairs, said that the goblin Tricky had advised him to buy them – and paid us for them straight away!'

'Who was he?' asked Peter, his heart sinking.

'Let me see – his name was Mr Spells,' said Polly, looking in a book. 'And his address is Wizard Cottage. He seemed very nice indeed.'

'Oh dear,' said Peter, leading Mollie out of the shop. 'Now we've *really* lost our dear old chair.'

'Don't give up!' said Mollie. 'We'll go back to Binky and tell him the whole story – and maybe he will know something about this Mr Spells and be able to get our chair back for us. Binky's very clever.'

'Yes – but before we can get it back from Mr Spells, that wretched goblin Tricky will be after it again,' said Peter. 'He's sure to go and take it from Mr Spells.'

The elf took them home again. They went into the playroom. Binky wasn't there! There was a note on the table.

It said: 'Fancy you going off without me! I've gone to look for you – Binky.'

'Bother!' said Mollie. 'How annoying! Here we've come back to look for him and he's gone to look for us. Now we'll have to wait till tomorrow!'

CHAPTER 5

OFF TO MR SPELLS OF WIZARD COTTAGE

Mollie and Peter certainly could do no more that day, because their mother was already wondering why they hadn't been in to tea. They heard her calling as they read Binky's note saying he had gone to look for them.

'It's a pity Binky didn't wait for us,' said Peter. 'We could have sent him to Mr Spells to keep guard on the chair. Come on, Mollie – we'll have to go in. We've hardly seen Mother all day!'

Their mother didn't know anything about the Wishing-Chair at all, of course, because the children kept it a strict secret.

'If we tell anyone, the grown-ups will come and take our precious chair and put it in a museum or something,' said Peter. 'I couldn't bear to think of the Wishing-Chair growing its wings in a museum and not being able to get out of a glass case.'

So they hadn't said a word to anyone. Now they ran indoors, and offered to help their mother shell peas. They sat and wondered where Binky was. They felt very sleepy, and Mollie suddenly gave an enormous yawn.

'You look very tired, Mollie,' said Mother, looking at her pale face. 'Didn't you sleep well last night?'

'Well – I didn't sleep a *lot*,' said Mollie truthfully, remembering her long flight in the Wishing-Chair and the strange bus ride afterwards.

'I think you had both better get off early to bed,' said Mother. 'I'll bring your suppers up to you in bed for a treat – raspberries and cream, and bread and butter – would you like that?'

In the ordinary way the children would have said no thank you to any idea of going to bed early – but they really were so sleepy that they both yawned together and said yes, that sounded nice, thank you, Mother!

So upstairs they went and fell asleep immediately after the raspberries and cream. Mother was really very surprised when she peeped in to see them.

'Poor children – I expect all the excitement of coming home from school has tired them out,' she said. 'I'll make them up sandwiches tomorrow and send them out on a picnic.'

They woke up early the next morning and their first thought was about the Wishing-Chair.

'Let's go down and see Binky,' said Mollie. 'We've got time before breakfast.'

So they dressed quickly and ran down to their playroom. But no Binky was there – and no note either. He hadn't been back, then. Wherever could he be?

'Oh dear, first the Wishing-Chair goes, and now Binky,' said Mollie. 'What's happened to him? I think we'd better go and ask that elf if he's seen him, Peter.'

'We shan't have time before breakfast,' said Peter. 'We'll come down as soon as we've done any jobs Mother wants us to do.'

They were both delighted when Mother suggested that they should take their lunch with them and go out for a day's picnicking. Why – that would be just right! They could go and hunt out the elf – and find Binky – and perhaps go to Mr Spells with him. Splendid!

So they eagerly took the packets of sandwiches, cake and chocolate that Mother made up for them, and Peter put them into a little satchel to carry. Off they went. They peeped into their playroom just to make sure that Binky still hadn't come back.

No, he hadn't. 'Better leave a note for him, then,' said Peter.

'What have you said?' asked Mollie, glancing over her shoulder.

'I've said: "Why didn't you wait for us, silly? Now we've got to go and look for you whilst you're still looking for us!"'

Mollie laughed. 'Oh dear – this really is getting ridiculous. Come on – let's go to the tree-house and see if the elf is in.'

So off they went, down the garden, through the hedge, and across the field to where the dark patch of grass was – the 'fairy ring.' They sat down in the middle of it and Mollie felt about for the button to press. She found something that felt like a little knob of earth and pressed it. Yes – it was the right button!

Down they went, not nearly as fast as the day before, because Mollie didn't press the button so hard. Then along the passage, past the strange bright little doors, and up the spiral stairway. They knocked on the door.

'It's us – Mollie and Peter. Can we come in?'

The door flew open and there stood the elf. He looked very pleased. 'Well, this is really friendly of you. Come in.'

'We've come to ask you something,' said Mollie. 'Have you seen Binky?'

'Oh, yes – he came to me yesterday, after I'd said goodbye to you, and I told him all you'd told me – and off he went to find Polly Polish and get the latest news,' said the elf.

'Well, he hasn't come back yet,' said Mollie. 'Where do you suppose he is!'

'Gone to see his mother, perhaps?' suggested the elf. 'I really don't know. It's not much good looking for him, really, you know – he might be anywhere.'

'Yes – that's true,' said Peter. 'Well, what shall we do, Mollie? Try and find Mr Spells of Wizard Cottage by ourselves?'

'Oh, I know where *he* lives,' said the elf. 'He's quite a nice fellow. I'll tell you the way. You want to take the bus through the Tall Hill, and then take the boat to the Mill. Not far off on the top of a hill you'll see a large cottage in the shape of a castle – only you can't call it a castle because it's not big enough. Mr Spells lives there.'

'Oh, thank you,' said Peter, and off they went to catch the bus. It was one like they had caught the other night, but it had a different driver, and was not nearly so crowded. In fact there would have been plenty of room inside for Peter and Mollie if they hadn't noticed that

34

one of the passengers happened to be Mr Sleep-Alone, Binky's strange and bad-tempered cousin.

'We'd better travel with the driver on the outside seat again,' said Peter. 'Sleep-Alone might recognise us and lose his temper again.'

The bus travelled fast down the lane, going round corners in a hair-raising style. 'Do you like going round corners on two wheels?' asked Peter, clutching at Mollie to prevent her from falling off.

'Well, it saves wear and tear on the others,' said the driver.

The bus suddenly ran straight at a very steep hill and disappeared into a black hole, which proved to be a long and bumpy tunnel. It came out again and stopped dead beside a little blue river, its front wheels almost touching the water.

'I always do that to give the passengers a fright,' said the driver. 'Must give them something for their money's worth!'

The children were really very glad to get out. They looked for a boat and saw plenty cruising about on the water, all by themselves. 'Look at that!' said Peter. 'They must go by magic or something.'

One little yellow boat sailed over to them and rocked gently beside them. They got into it. The boat didn't move.

'Tell it where to go, silly!' called the bus-driver, who was watching them with great interest.

'To the Mill,' said Peter, and immediately the boat shot off downstream, doing little zigzags now and again in a very light-hearted manner. It wasn't long before they came to an old Mill. Its big water-wheel was working and made a loud noise. Behind it was a hill, and on the top was what looked like a small castle.

'That's where Mr Spells lives,' said Peter. 'Come on – out we get, and up the hill we go.'

So up the hill they went and came at last to the curious castle-like house.

But when they got near they heard loud shouts and thumps and yells, and they stopped in alarm.

'Whatever's going on?' said Mollie. 'Is somebody quarrelling?'

The children tiptoed to the house and peeped in at one of the windows, the one where the noise seemed to be coming from. They saw a peculiar sight!

Binky and a nasty-looking little goblin seemed to be playing musical chairs! The children saw the six chairs there that they had seen the day before in Mr Polish's shop, and first Binky would dart at one and look at it carefully and try to pull it away, and then the goblin would. Then Mr Spells, who looked a very grand kind of enchanter, would pull the chairs away from each and then threaten both the goblin and Binky with his stick.

Roars and bellows came from the goblin and howls from Binky. Oh dear. Whatever was happening?

'Binky must have found out that the chairs had gone to Mr Spells, and gone to get our own chair,' said Peter. 'And the goblin must have gone to get it at the same time. Can you see the blue handkerchief we tied on our own chair, Mollie?'

'No. It's gone. Somebody took it off,' said Mollie. 'I believe I can see it sticking out of Binky's pocket – I expect he guessed we marked the chair that way and took the hanky off in case the goblin or Mr Spells guessed there was something unusual about that particular chair.'

'Sir!' cried Binky suddenly, turning to Mr Spells, 'I tell you once more that I am only here to fetch back one of these chairs, a wishing-chair, which belongs to me and my friends. This goblin stole it from us – and now he's come to get it back again from you. He'll sell it again, and steal it – he's a bad fellow.'

The goblin thumped Binky and he yelled. Mr Spells roared like a lion. 'I don't believe either of you. You're a couple of rogues. These chairs are MY CHAIRS, all of them, and I don't believe any of them is a wishing-chair. Wishing-chairs have wings, and not one of these has.'

'But I tell you . . .' began Binky, and then stopped as the enchanter struck him lightly with his wand, and then struck the goblin too.

Binky sank down into a deep sleep and so did the goblin. 'Now I shall have a little peace at last,' said Mr Spells. 'And I'll find out which chair is a wishing-chair – if these fellows are speaking the truth!'

He went out of the room, and the children heard him stirring something somewhere. He was probably making a Find-Out Spell!

'Come on – let's get into the room and drag Binky out whilst he's gone,' said Peter. 'We simply must rescue him!'

So they crept in through the window and bent over

Binky. And just at that very moment they felt a strong draught blowing round them!

They looked at each of the chairs – yes, one of them had grown wings, and was flapping them, making quite a wind! Hurray – now they could fly off in the Wishing-Chair, and cram Binky in with them, fast asleep.

'Quick, oh, quick – Mr Spells is coming back!'said Peter. 'Help me with Binky – quick, Mollie, QUICK!'

CHAPTER 6

MR SPELLS IS VERY MAGIC

The Wishing-Chair stood with the other five chairs, its red wings flapping strongly. The children caught hold of the sleeping pixie and dragged him to the chair. He felt as heavy as lead! If only he would wake up.

'He's in a terribly magic sleep,' said Mollie in despair. 'Now – lift him, Peter – that's right – and put him safely on the seat of the chair. Oh dear, he's rolling off again. Do, do be quick!'

They could hear Mr Spells muttering in the next room, stirring something in a pot. In a few moments he would have made his Find-Out Spell to see which was the Wishing-Chair, and would come back into the room. They *must* get away first!

The chair's wings were now fully grown, and it was doing little hops on the ground as if it were impatient to be off. The children sat down in it, holding Binky tightly. Tricky the goblin was still lying on the floor, fast asleep. Good!

'Fly home, Chair, fly home!' commanded Peter. Just in time too, because as he spoke the children could hear the wizard's steps coming towards them from the next room. He appeared at the door, carrying something in a shining bottle.

The chair had now risen in the air, flapping its wings, and was trying to get out of the window. It was an awkward shape for the chair to get through, and it turned itself sideways so that the children and Binky almost fell out! They clung to the arms in fright, trying to stop Binky from rolling off.

'Hey!' cried the wizard in the greatest astonishment. 'What are you doing? Why, the chair's grown wings! Who are you, children – and what are you doing with my chair? Come back.'

But by this time the chair was out of the window and was the right way up again, much to the children's relief. It flew up into the air.

'Good! We've escaped – and we've got both the chair *and* Binky,' said Peter, pleased. 'Even if he is asleep, we've got him. We'll have to ask the elf if he knows how to wake him up.'

But Peter spoke too soon. Mr Spells was too clever to let the chair escape quite so easily. He came running out into the little garden in front of his castle-like cottage, carrying something over his arm.

'What's he going to do?' said Mollie. 'What's he got, Peter?'

They soon knew! It was a very, very long rope, with a loop at the end to lasso them with! Mr Spells swung the loops of rope round for a second or two, then flung the rope up into the air. The loops unwound and the last loop of all almost touched them. But not quite! The chair gave a jump of fright and rose a little higher.

'Oh, do go quickly, Chair!' begged Mollie. 'The

wizard is gathering up the rope to throw it again. Look out – here it comes! Oh, Peter, it's going to catch us – it's longer than ever!'

The rope sped up to them like a long, thin snake. The last loop of all fell neatly round the chair, but, before it could tighten, Peter caught hold of it and threw it off. He really did it very cleverly indeed.

'Oh, Peter – you *are* marvellous!' cried Mollie. 'I really thought we were caught that time. Surely we are out of reach now – the wizard looks very small and far away.'

Once more the rope came flying towards the Wishing-Chair, and it tried to dodge it, almost upsetting the children altogether. The rope darted after the chair, fell firmly round it – and before Peter could throw it off it had tightened itself round the chair and the children too!

Peter struggled hard to get a knife to cut the rope – but his arms were pinned tightly to his sides and he couldn't put his hands into his pockets. Mollie tried to help him, but it was no use. Mr Spells was hauling on the rope and the chair was going gradually down and down and down.

'Oh dear – we're caught!' said Mollie in despair. 'Just when we had so nearly escaped too! Peter, do think of something.'

But Peter couldn't. Binky might have been able to think of some spell to get rid of the rope but he was still fast asleep. Mollie had to use both hands to hold him on the chair in case he fell off.

Down went the chair, pulling against the rope and making things as difficult as possible for the wizard, who was in a fine old temper when at last he had the chair on the ground.

'What do you mean by this?' he said sternly. 'What kind of behaviour is this – coming to my house, stealing one of the chairs I bought – the Wishing-Chair too, the best of the lot? I didn't even know one of the chairs was a magic chair when I bought the set.'

Mollie was almost crying. Peter looked sulky as he tried to free his arms from the tight rope.

'You'll keep that rope round you for the rest of the day,' said Mr Spells. 'Just to teach you that you can't steal from a wizard.'

'Let me free,' said Peter. 'I'm not a thief, and I

haven't stolen this chair – unless you call taking something that really belongs to us *stealing*. I don't!'

'What do you mean?' said Mr Spells. 'I'm tired of hearing people say this chair is theirs. Tricky said it – Binky said it – and now you say it! It can't belong to all of you – and, anyway, I bought it with my money.'

'Mr Spells, this Wishing-Chair is ours,' said Peter patiently. 'It lives in our playroom, and Binky the pixie shares it with us and looks after it. Tricky stole it and sold it to Mr Polish, who had five other chairs like it.'

'And then Tricky told you about the six old chairs and you went and bought them,' said Mollie. 'And Tricky came tonight to get back the Wishing-Chair because it's valuable and he can sell it to somebody else!'

'And then Binky came to try and tell you about it before Tricky stole it,' went on Peter. 'And I suppose they came at the same time and quarrelled about it.'

'Well, well!' said Mr Spells, who had been listening in surprise. 'This is a strange story, I must say. It's true that I came in from the garden to find the goblin and the pixie behaving most peculiarly. They kept sitting down first on one chair and then on another – trying to find out which was the Wishing-Chair, I suppose – and shouting at one another all the time.'

'I'd tied my blue hanky on the right arm of the Wishing-Chair,' said Mollie.

'Yes – I saw it there and wondered why,' said Mr Spells. 'I can see it in Binky's pocket now – he must have recognised it as yours and taken it off. Well, I suppose you came in just at the moment when I was angry with them both, and put them into a magic sleep.'

'Yes,' said Peter. 'Then you went out and we thought we'd escape if we could, taking Binky with us. The chair suddenly grew its wings, you see.'

'Mr Spells, can we have back our chair, please, now that you've heard our story?' begged Mollie. 'I know you've paid some money to Mr Polish for it – but couldn't you get it back from Tricky the goblin? After all, he's the rogue in all this, isn't he – not us or Binky?'

'You're quite right,' said Mr Spells. 'And I think it was very brave of you to come to rescue Binky. I'm sorry I put him into a magic sleep now – but I'll wake him up again. And now I'll take the rope off and set you free!'

He took the rope off Peter and then lifted Binky from the Wishing-Chair and laid him down on the floor. He drew a white ring of chalk round him and then a ring of blue inside the white circle. Then he called loudly.

'Cinders! Where are you? Dear me, that cat is never about when he's wanted!'

There was a loud miaow outside the window. In jumped a big black cat with green eyes that shone like traffic signals! He ran to Mr Spells.

'Cinders, I'm going to do a wake-up spell,' said the wizard. 'Go and sit in the magic ring and sing with me whilst I chant the spell.'

Cinders leapt lightly over the chalk rings and sat down close to the sleeping Binky. Mr Spells began to walk round and round, just outside the ring, chanting a curious song. It sounded like: –

> 'Birriloola-kummi-pool,
> Rimminy, romminy, rye,
> Tibbynooka-falli-lool,
> Open your sleepy eye!'

All the time the wizard chanted this strange song the cat kept up a loud miaowing as if he were joining in too.

The spell was a very good one, because at the end of the chant, Binky opened first one eye and then the other. He sat up, looking extremely surprised.

'I say,' he began, 'what's happened? Where am I? Oh, hallo, Peter and Mollie! I've been looking for you everywhere!'

'And *we've* been looking for you!' said Mollie. 'You've been in a magic sleep. Get up and come home with us. The Wishing-Chair has grown its wings again.'

Then Binky saw Mr Spells standing nearby, tall and commanding, and he went rather pale. 'But, I say – what does Mr Spells think about all this?' he said, nervously.

'I have heard the children's story and it is quite plain that the chair really does belong to you,' he said. 'I'll get the money back from Tricky.'

'Well, he's *very* tricky, so be careful of him,' said Binky, sitting down in the Wishing-Chair with the children.

'He'll get a shock when he wakes up,' said Mr Spells, and he suddenly touched the sleeping goblin with the toe of his foot. 'Dimini, dimini, dimini, diminish!' he cried suddenly, and lo and behold the goblin shrank

45

swiftly to a very tiny creature indeed, diminishing rapidly before the astonished eyes of the watching children.

Mr Spells picked up the tiny goblin, took a matchbox off the mantelpiece, popped him into it, shut the box and put it back on the mantelpiece.

'He won't cause me any trouble when he wakes up!' he said. 'No, not a bit! Well, goodbye. I'm glad this has all ended well – but I do wish that chair was mine.'

The children waved goodbye and the chair rose into the air. 'Shall we go home?' said Peter.

'No,' said Mollie, suddenly remembering the satchel of sandwiches and cake that Peter still carried. 'We'll take Binky off for the day, picnicking! We deserve a nice peaceful day after such a thrilling adventure.'

'Right!' said Peter, and Binky nodded happily. 'Wishing-Chair, take us to the nicest picnic spot you know!' And off they flew at once, to have a very happy day together.

CHAPTER 7

OFF ON ANOTHER ADVENTURE!

For a whole week the children watched and waited for the Wishing-Chair to grow its wings again. It didn't sprout them at all! The wings had vanished as soon as it had arrived safely back in the playroom.

'I hope its magic isn't getting less,' said Mollie, one day, as they sat in the playroom, playing ludo together. It was their very favourite game, and they always laughed at Binky because he made such a fuss when he didn't get 'home' before they did.

As they sat playing together they felt a welcome draught. 'Oh, lovely! A breeze at last!' said Mollie thankfully. 'I do really think this is just about the hottest day we've had these holidays!'

'The wind must have got up a bit at last,' said Peter. 'Blow, wind, blow – you are making us lovely and cool.'

'Funny that the leaves on the trees aren't moving, isn't it?' said Binky.

Mollie looked out of the open door at the trees in the garden. They were perfectly still! 'But there *isn't* a breeze,' she said, and then a sudden thought struck her. She looked round at the Wishing-Chair, which was standing just behind them.

'Look!' she cried. 'How silly we are! It isn't the wind – it's the Wishing-Chair that has grown its wings again. They are flapping like anything!'

So they were. The children and Binky sprang up in delight. 'Good! We could just do with a lovely cool ride up in the air today,' said Peter. 'Wishing-Chair, we are very pleased with you!'

The Wishing-Chair flapped its wings very strongly again and gave a creak. Then Binky noticed something.

'I say, look – it's only grown *three* wings instead of four. What's happened? It's never done that before.'

They all stared at the chair. One of its front legs hadn't grown a wing. It looked rather odd without it.

Binky looked at the chair rather doubtfully. 'Do you think it can fly with only three wings?' he said. 'This is rather a peculiar thing to happen, really. I wonder if we ought to fly off in the chair if it's only got three wings instead of four.'

'I don't see why not,' said Mollie. 'After all, an aeroplane can fly with three engines, if the fourth one stops.'

The chair gave a little hop up in the air as if to say it could fly perfectly well. 'Oh, come along!' said Binky. 'We'll try. I'm sure it will be all right. But I wish I knew what to do to get the fourth wing to grow. Something has gone wrong, it's plain.'

They got into the chair, Binky as usual sitting on the back, holding on to their shoulders. The chair flew to the door.

'Where shall we go?' said Binky.

'Well – we never did get to the Land of Goodness Knows Where after all,' said Mollie. 'Shall we try to get there again? We know it's a good way away, so it should be a nice long flight, very cool and windy high up in the air.'

'We may as well,' said Binky. 'Fly to the Land of Goodness Knows Where, Chair. We saw it on the map – it's due east from here, straight towards where the sun rises – you go over the Tiptop Mountains, past the Crazy Valley and then down by the Zigzag Coast.'

'It sounds exciting,' said Mollie. 'Oh, isn't it lovely to be cool again? It's so very hot today.'

They were now high up in the air, and a lovely breeze blew past them as they flew. Little clouds, like puffs of cotton wool, floated below them. Mollie leaned out to get hold of one as they passed.

'This is fun,' she said. 'Binky, is there a land of ice-creams? If so, I'd like to go there sometime!'

'I don't know. I've never heard of one,' said Binky. 'There's a Land of Goodies though, I know that. It once came to the top of the Faraway Tree, and I went there. It was lovely – biscuits growing on trees, and chocolates sprouting on bushes.'

'Oh – did you see Moon-Face and Silky and the old Saucepan Man?' asked Mollie, in excitement. 'I've read the books about the Faraway Tree, and I've always wished I could climb it.'

'Yes, I saw them all,' said Binky. 'Silky is sweet, you'd love her. But Moon-Face was cross because somebody had taken all his slippery-slip cushions – you know, the cushions he keeps in his room at the top of the tree for people to sit on when they slide down from the top to the bottom.'

'I wouldn't mind going to the Land of Goodies at all,' said Peter. 'It sounds really fine. I almost wish we'd told the chair to go there instead of the Land of Goodness Knows Where.'

'Well, don't change its mind for it,' said Binky. 'It doesn't like that. Look, there are the Tip top Mountains.'

They all leaned out to look. They were very extraordinary mountains, running up into high, jagged peaks as if somebody had drawn them higgledy-piggledy with a pencil, up and down, up and down.

On they went, through a batch of tiny little clouds; but Mollie didn't try to catch any of these because, just in time, she saw that baby elves were fast asleep on them, one to each cloud.

'They make good cradles for a hot day like this,' explained Binky.

After a while, Mollie noticed that Binky was leaning rather hard on her shoulder, and that Peter seemed to be leaning against her too. She pushed them back.

'Don't lean so heavily on me,' she said.

'We don't mean to,' said Peter. 'But I seem to be leaning that way all the time! I do try not to.'

'Why are we, I wonder?' said Binky. Then he gave a cry. 'Why, the chair's all on one side. No wonder Peter and I keep going over on to you, Mollie. Look – it's tipped sideways!'

'What's the matter with it?' said Mollie. She tried to

shake the chair upright by swinging herself about in it, but it always overbalanced to the left side as soon as she had stopped swinging it to and fro.

They all looked in alarm at one another as the chair began to tip more and more to one side. It was very difficult to sit in it when it tipped like that.

'It's because it's only got three wings!' said Binky, suddenly. 'Of course that's it! The one wing on this side is tired out, and so the chair is flying with only two wings really, and it's tipping over. It will soon be on its side in the air!'

'Gracious! Then for goodness' sake let's go down to the ground at once,' said Mollie, in alarm. 'We shall fall out if we don't.'

'Go down to the ground, Chair,' commanded Peter, feeling the chair going over to one side even more. He looked over the side. The one wing there had already stopped flapping. The chair was using only two wings – they would soon be tired out too!

The chair flew heavily down to the ground and landed with rather a bump. Its wings stopped flapping and hung limp. It creaked dolefully. It was quite exhausted, that was plain!

'We shouldn't have flown off on it when it only had three wings,' said Binky. 'It was wrong of us. After all, Peter and Mollie, you have grown bigger since last holidays, and must be heavier. The chair can't possibly take us all unless it has *four* wings to fly with.'

They stood and looked at the poor, tired Wishing-Chair. 'What are we going to do about it?' said Peter.

'Well – we must try to find out where we are first,' said Binky, looking round. 'And then we must ask if there is a witch or wizard or magician anywhere about that can give us something to make the chair grow another wing. Then we'd better take it straight home for a rest.'

'Look,' said Mollie, pointing to a nearby signpost. 'It says "To the Village of Slipperies". Do you know that village, Binky?'

'No. But I've heard of it,' said Binky. 'The people there aren't very nice – slippery as eels – can't trust them or believe a word they say. I don't think we'll go that way.'

He went to look at the other arm of the signpost and came back looking very pleased.

'It says "Dame Quick-Fingers",' he said. 'She's my great-aunt. She'll help us all right. She'll be sure to know a spell for growing wings. She keeps a pack of flying dogs, you know, because of the Slipperies – they simply fly after them when they come to steal her chickens and ducks.'

'Goodness – I'd love to see some flying dogs,' said Mollie. 'Where does this aunt of yours live?'

'Just down the road, round a corner, and by a big rowan tree,' said Binky. 'She's really nice. I dare say she'd ask us to tea if we are as polite as possible. She loves good manners.'

'Well – you go and ask her if she knows how to grow an extra wing on our chair,' said Mollie. 'We'd better stay here with the chair, I think, in case anyone thinks of stealing it again. We can easily bring it along to your aunt's cottage, if she's in. We won't carry it all the way there in case she's not.'

'Right. I'll go,' said Binky. 'I won't be long. You just sit in the chair till I come back – and don't you let anyone steal it.'

He ran off down the road and disappeared round a corner. Mollie and Peter sat down in the chair to wait. The chair creaked. It sounded very tired indeed. Mollie patted its arms. 'You'll soon be all right once you have got a fourth wing,' she said. 'Cheer up.'

Binky hadn't been gone very long before the sound of footsteps made the children look round. Five little people were coming along the road from the Village of Slipperies. They looked most peculiar.

'They must be Slipperies,' said Peter, sitting up. 'Now we must be careful they don't play a trick on us and get the chair away. Aren't they odd-looking?'

The five little creatures came up and bowed low. 'Good day,' they said. 'We come to greet you and to ask you to visit our village.'

CHAPTER 8
THE SLIPPERIES PLAY A TRICK!

Peter and Mollie looked hard at the five Slipperies.
Each Slippery had one blue eye and one green, and not
one of them looked straight at the children! Their hair
was slick and smooth, their mouths smiled without
stopping, and they rubbed their bony hands together all
the time.

'I'm sorry,' said Peter, 'but we don't want to leave our
chair. We're waiting here with it till our friend Binky
comes back from seeing his Great-Aunt Quick-Fingers.'

'Oh, she's gone to market,' said one of the Slipperies.
'She always goes on Thursdays.'

'Oh dear,' said Peter. 'How tiresome! Now we shan't
be able to get a fourth wing for our Wishing-Chair.'

'Dear me – is this a Wishing-Chair?' said the
Slipperies, in great interest. 'It's the first time we've
seen one. Do let us sit in it.'

'Certainly not,' said Peter, feeling certain that if he let
them sit in the chair they would try to fly off in it.

'I hear that Great-Aunt Quick-Fingers has some
flying dogs,' said Mollie, hoping that the Slipperies would
look frightened at the mention of them. But they didn't.

They rubbed their slippery hands together again and

went on smiling. 'Ah, yes – wonderful dogs they are. If you stand up on your chair, and look over the field yonder, you may see some of them flying around,' said one Slippery.

The children stood on the seat of the chair. The Slipperies clustered round them. 'Now look right down over that field,' began one of them. 'Do you see a tall tree?'

'Yes,' said Mollie.

'Well, look to the right of it and you'll see the roof of a house. And then to the right of that and you'll see another tree,' said the Slippery.

'Can't you tell me *exactly* where to look?' said Mollie, getting impatient. 'I can't see a single flying dog. Only a rook or two.'

'Well, now look to the left and . . .' began another Slippery, when Peter jumped down from the chair.

'You're just making it all up,' he said. 'Go on, be off with you! I don't like any of you.'

The Slipperies lost their smiles, and looked nasty. They laid hands on the Wishing-Chair.

'I shall whistle for the flying dogs,' said Peter suddenly. 'Now let me see – what is the whistle, ah, yes . . .' And he suddenly whistled a very shrill whistle indeed.

The Slipperies shot off at once as if a hundred of the flying dogs were after them! Mollie laughed.

'Peter! That's not really a whistle for flying dogs, is it?'

'No, of course not. But I had to get rid of them somehow,' said Peter. 'I had a feeling they were going to trick us with their silly smiles and rubbing hands and odd eyes – so I had to think of some way of tricking *them* instead.'

'I wish Binky would come,' said Mollie, sitting down in the chair again. 'He's been ages. And it's all a waste of time, his going to find his great-aunt, if she's at the market. We shall have to go there, I expect, and carry the chair all the way.'

'Why, there *is* Binky!' said Peter, waving. 'Oh, good, he's dancing and smiling. He's got the spell to make another wing grow.'

'Then his great-aunt couldn't have gone to market!' said Mollie. 'Hey, Binky! Have you got the spell? Was your Great-Aunt Quick-Fingers in?'

'Yes – and awfully pleased to see me,' said Binky, running up. 'And she gave me just enough magic to make another wing grow, so we shan't be long now.'

'Five Slipperies came up, and they said your great-aunt always goes to market on Thursdays,' said Mollie.

'You can't believe a word they say,' said Binky. 'I told you that. My word, I'm glad they didn't trick you in any way. They usually trick everyone, no matter how clever they may be.'

'Well, they didn't trick *us*,' said Peter. 'We were much too smart for them – weren't we, Mollie?'

'Yes. They wanted to sit in the chair when they knew it was a Wishing-Chair,' said Mollie. 'But we wouldn't let them.'

'I should think not,' said Binky. He showed the children a little blue box. 'Look – I've got a smear of ointment here that is just enough to grow a red wing to match the other wings. Then the chair will be quite all right.'

'Well, let's rub it on,' said Peter. Binky knelt down by the chair – and then he gave a cry of horror.

'What's the matter?' said the children.

'Look – somebody has cut off the other three wings of the chair!' groaned Binky. 'Cut them right off short. There's only a stump left of each.'

Mollie and Peter stared in horror. Sure enough the other three wings had been cut right off. But how? And when? Who could have done it? The children had been with the chair the whole time.

'I do think you might have kept a better guard on the chair,' said Binky crossly. 'I really do. Didn't I warn you about the ways of the Slipperies? Didn't I say you couldn't trust them? Didn't I . . .'

'Oh, Binky – but when could it have been done?' cried Mollie. 'I tell you, we were here the whole of the time.'

'Standing by the chair?' asked Binky.

'Yes – or *on* it,' said Peter.

'*On* it! Whatever did you stand *on* it, for?' said Binky, puzzled. 'To stop the Slipperies sitting down?'

'No – to see your great-aunt's flying-dogs,' said Peter. 'The Slipperies said they were over there, and if we would stand up on the chair seat we could just see them flying around. But we couldn't.'

'Of course you couldn't,' said Binky. 'And for a very good reason too – they're all at the cottage with my great-aunt. I saw them!'

'Oh – the dreadful story-tellers!' cried Mollie. 'Peter – it was a trick! Whilst we were standing up there trying to see the dogs, one of the Slipperies must have quietly snipped off the three wings and put them in his pocket.'

'Of course!' said Binky. 'Very simple – and you're a pair of simpletons to get taken in by such a silly trick.'

Mollie and Peter went very red. 'What shall we do?' asked Peter. 'I'm very sorry about it. Poor old chair – one wing not grown and the other three snipped away. It's a shame.'

'Thank goodness Binky has the Growing Ointment for wings,' said Mollie.

'Yes – but I've only got just enough for *one* wing,' said Binky. 'One wing isn't going to take us very far, is it?'

'No,' said Mollie. 'Whatever are we going to do?'

'I shall have to ask Great-Aunt Quick-Fingers for

some more Growing Ointment, that's all,' said Binky, gloomily. 'And this time you can come with me, *and* bring the chair too. If I leave you here alone with it, you'll get tricked again, and I shall come back and find the *legs* are gone next time, and I can't even grow wings on them!'

'It's not nice of you to keep on and on about it, Binky,' said Mollie, lifting up the chair with Peter. 'We're very sorry. We didn't know quite how clever the Slipperies were. Oooh – horrid creatures, with their odd eyes and deceitful smiles.'

They followed Binky down the road and along a lane. Soon he came to his great-aunt's cottage. It was very snug and small. To Mollie's enormous delight, five or six little brown dogs, rather like spaniels were flying about the garden on small white wings. They barked loudly and flew to the three of them.

'Now, now – these are friends of mine,' said Binky, and patted the nearest dog, which was flying round his head.

It was strange to have the little dogs sailing about the air like gulls! One flew up to Mollie and rested its front paws on her shoulder. She laughed, and the dog licked her face. Then off it flew again, and chased after a sparrow, barking madly.

Great-Aunt Quick-Fingers came to the door, looking surprised. 'Why, Binky – back again so soon!' she said. 'What's happened?'

Binky told her. 'So you see, Great-Aunt, now that the poor chair has lost *all* its wings, I'm afraid that the Growing Ointment you gave me won't be enough,' said

Binky. 'I'm so sorry.'

'Well, well – it takes a very clever person to see through the Slippery ways,' said his great-aunt. 'You'd better come in and have tea now you're all here!'

The children put down the Wishing-Chair and Great-Aunt Quick-Fingers got the little treacle tarts out of the oven. 'There you are,' she said. 'Get your fingers nice and sticky with those! I'll go and make some more Growing Ointment for you. It won't take long.'

She disappeared, and the children sat and munched the lovely treacle tarts.

Just at that moment she came back, with a fairly large jar. She handed it to Binky. 'There you are. Use that and see what happens. But remember, you can only use it once on anything. The spell doesn't act twice. It's no good trying to use the ointment another time on the chair, to make it grow wings, because it won't be any use.'

Binky dipped his finger into the jar of ointment. It was curious stuff, bright yellow with green streaks in it.

He rubbed some on to a chair leg and immediately a most wonderful wing sprouted out, big and strong!

'I say – it isn't red, as it always is!' cried Mollie. 'It's green and yellow – and a much bigger wing than before. I say, Chair, you *will* look grand. Make another wing come, Binky.'

Soon the Wishing-Chair had four grand green and yellow wings, much bigger than its old red ones. It waved them about proudly.

'You'd better get in the chair and go before it tries its new wings out by itself,' said Great-Aunt Quick-

Fingers. So in they all got, Binky on the back, as usual – and off they went!

'Home, Chair, home!' cried everyone, and it rose high in the air, and flew off to the west. 'Goodbye and thank you very much,' cried Binky and the children, and Great-Aunt waved till they were out of sight.

'Well, that was quite a nice little adventure,' said Peter. 'And the chair's got some wonderful new wings. I do hope they'll always grow like this in future – big and strong, and all green and yellow!'

CHAPTER 9

MOLLIE AND THE GROWING OINTMENT

The children were very pleased with the chair's beautiful new green and yellow wings. 'They're much better than the little red ones it used to grow,' said Peter. 'Your great-aunt's Growing Ointment is marvellous stuff, Binky. I only hope the chair will grow its wings more often now.'

The green and yellow wings disappeared, of course, as soon as they were all safely at home again. The chair stood still in its place, looking quite ordinary. The children patted it.

'Good old Wishing-Chair. Grow your wings again soon. You haven't taken us to the Land of Goodness Knows Where yet, you know!'

The chair didn't grow its wings again that week. Friday came, Saturday, Sunday, Monday. The children grew tired of asking Binky if the chair was growing its wings yet.

On Tuesday a spell of rainy weather began. It really was too wet to play any games out of doors at all. The children went down to their playroom day after day to play with Binky, and that was fun. But on Friday Binky said he really must go and see how his dear old mother was.

'I haven't seen her since I came back to you with the chair,' he said. 'I must go today.'

'Oh, bother! We shall have to do without you,' said Mollie. 'Just suppose the chair grows its wings, Binky, and you're not here.'

'Well, that's easy,' said Binky, with a grin. 'Simply sit in it and wish it to go to my mother's. She will be very pleased to see you, and then we can all three of us go adventuring somewhere.'

'Oh, yes – we'll do that, if only the chair grows wings,' said Peter. 'Well, goodbye, Binky. Will you be back tonight?'

'Yes,' said Binky. 'I'll be sleeping on the old sofa as usual, don't worry. I'm not taking my wand with me, by the way, so keep an eye on it, will you?'

Binky had just bought a new wand, a very useful one that had quite a bit of magic in it. He was very proud of it, and kept it in the cupboard with the toys and games.

'Yes – we'll look after it for you,' said Peter. 'And we won't use it, we promise.'

'I know you won't,' said Binky. 'Well, see you tonight.'

Off he went to catch the bus to his mother's cottage, dressed in his mackintosh and sou'wester. The children felt decidedly dull when he had gone.

'Game of ludo, Mollie?' said Peter.

'No. I'm bored with ludo today,' said Mollie.

'Well, you're not going to be very good company, then,' said Peter, taking down a book. 'I'll read. You can tell me when you've finished being bored and we'll think up an exciting game.'

Mollie lay down on the rug and shut her eyes. What a pity it had rained and rained so long. Even if the Wishing-Chair grew its wings, it wouldn't be much fun going out in the rain. They would have to take an umbrella with them.

Mollie opened her eyes and looked out of the window. Why, the sun was shining – and yet it was still raining.

'I say, Peter, look at this rainbow,' said Mollie. 'It's glorious. Oh – wouldn't it be lovely to fly off to a rainbow in the Wishing-Chair! If it looks as beautiful as this far away, whatever would it look like very near to us? Oh, I do wish the Wishing-Chair would grow its wings this very afternoon.'

Peter took no notice. He was deep in his book. Mollie felt cross. She wandered round the room and opened a little cupboard where Binky kept some of his things. There on the shelf was the jar of Growing Ointment that Great-Aunt Quick-Fingers had given him to make the wings of the Wishing-Chair sprout again.

Mollie took down the jar and opened the lid. There was plenty of ointment left – yellow with streaks of green in it. She wondered if perhaps it *would* make the chair's wings grow again, although Binky's great-aunt had said it only acted once on anything.

'I'll try it,' thought Mollie. 'And I won't tell Peter! If the wings grow, I'll fly off in the Wishing-Chair without him, and go to Binky's alone. That will serve him right for not answering when I speak to him!'

She went over to the Wishing-Chair and rubbed a

little of the ointment on one of the front legs. Nothing happened at all. She couldn't feel even a tiny bud of a wing beginning to grow; the Growing Ointment certainly didn't act twice. Great-Aunt Quick-Fingers was right.

Then a wonderful thought came to Mollie. Why shouldn't she try a little of the magic ointment on something else? She looked round. Her dolls, for instance! Oh, if only she could make wings grow on Rosebud, her prettiest doll. That would be really wonderful.

Feeling very excited, Mollie took her doll Rosebud from her cot. She rubbed a little of the green and yellow ointment on to her back – and, hey presto! wing-buds began to form – and little green and yellow wings sprouted out on the doll's back.

And she suddenly left Mollie's knee and flew – yes, *flew* – round the playroom. She flew near Peter and he felt the wind of her little wings. He looked up – and his eyes almost dropped out of his head as he saw Rosebud flying gaily round the room!

Mollie laughed in delight and tried to catch the doll as she flew past. 'I've put some of the Growing Ointment on her back,' she said. 'You know – what Binky's great-aunt gave him for growing wings on the Wishing-Chair. And Rosebud grew wings!'

'Well, I never!' said Peter in amazement. 'I say – do you think my engine would grow wings too?' he said suddenly. He had a wonderful clockwork engine, a perfect model that he was very proud of.

'Oh, *yes* – let's try and see,' said Mollie. So they got the engine and Peter smeared a little of the ointment on to it. It sprouted out small wings at once!

It flew from Peter's hand and joined the doll. The children laughed till their sides ached to see the two toys behaving like this. They really did look extraordinary.

And then Mollie and Peter went quite mad with the ointment. They smeared it on to a top and that flew round the room, spinning as it went! They smeared the skittles and they all shot round and round, some of them bumping into one another in the air.

They made some of the little toy soldiers fly, and they even gave the bricks in their brick box wings to fly with. All these things flapped their way round the room, and Mollie and Peter screamed with laughter as they tried to dodge the flying toys.

Mollie went to the toy cupboard to see if any toy was there that could be made to fly as well. She picked up Binky's new wand and put it on one side – but, dear me, her fingers were smeared with the Growing Ointment and the wand at once grew tiny, graceful green and yellow wings too! It flew out of the cupboard and joined the flying toys.

'Oh dear – there goes the wand,' said Mollie. 'I do hope Binky won't mind. I just touched it by accident with the ointment smeared on my fingers, and it grew wings.'

'Look – I've made the teapot fly,' said Peter, and roared with laughter to see it flapping its way round the room. 'Look at the skittles colliding again.'

The wind suddenly blew the door wide open. Then a

dreadful thing happened. Rosebud the doll, the railway engine, the skittles, the bricks, the top, the teapot, the wand; in fact everything that had grown wings shot straight out of the open door, flew down to the bottom of the garden and vanished!

'Ooooh!' said Mollie in fright.

'They've gone,' said Peter, and rushed to the open door. But he could see nothing. No Rosebud was there, no engine, nothing. They had all vanished into the blue.

'Oh dear – shall we get them back?' said Mollie. 'Why did I ever begin to smear the Growing Ointment on anything? It was a very silly idea. Now I've lost Rosebud.'

'And what about my lovely model engine?' said Peter. 'And I *say* – Binky's magic wand has gone too!'

They stared at one another in dismay. Binky's new wand, that he had saved up for and was so proud of! It had grown wings and now it had flown out of the door and vanished too. This was dreadful.

'We shall have to tell Binky when he gets back tonight, and ask him if we can possibly get the things back,' said Mollie. 'If we knew where they had gone we could go and fetch them. Do you suppose they've gone to Great-Aunt Quick-Fingers?'

They said no more to one another, but sat solemnly side by side, hoping and hoping that the things would fly back as unexpectedly as they had flown away. But they didn't.

Binky came back at half-past six, looking very merry and bright, and bringing a big chocolate cake from his mother. He stopped when he saw their doleful faces.

'What's up?' he said. 'Anything happened?'

They told him, and Binky listened in astonishment. He leapt to his feet when they spoke about his wand.

'WHAT! You don't mean to tell me you were silly enough to meddle with my wand – surely you didn't make my *wand* grow wings too!'

'It was an accident,' said poor Mollie. 'I must have had some of the ointment on my fingers when I moved it – and so it grew wings too. I'm so sorry, Binky.'

'Where have the things gone, Binky?' asked Peter.

'I don't know,' said Binky. 'I haven't the least idea. All I can say is – the next time the Wishing-Chair grows its wings, we'll have to tell it to go wherever the toys have gone – but goodness knows where it will take us to!'

CHAPTER 10
OFF TO FIND THE TOYS

Binky was gloomy and cross that evening. The children were sad, and felt ashamed that they had gone quite so mad with the Growing Ointment. They felt very guilty indeed about Binky's wand.

'Will you come and tell us if the Wishing-Chair grows its wings again tonight, Binky?' asked Mollie when it was time for them to go back to the house.

'I might,' said Binky gruffly. 'And I might not. I might go off by myself in it.'

'Oh, no, don't do that,' begged Mollie. 'That would be horrid of you. Dear Binky, please be nice and forgive us for losing your wand.'

'All right,' said Binky, cheering up a little.

'I really do feel very upset about losing my doll Rosebud, you know,' went on poor Mollie. 'I feel just as upset about her as you feel about your wand.'

'And I'm miserable about my engine,' said Peter. 'It was the finest I ever had.'

'Well – we'll hope the Wishing-Chair grows its wings again tonight, then, and we can go and fetch everything,' said Binky. 'I'll come and tap on your windows if it grows its wings.'

But Binky didn't tap on their windows at all. The chair didn't grow any wings in the night. Mollie sighed.

'Just when we so badly want it to fly, it won't grow wings! Now today we've got to behave nicely and be on our best behaviour, because Mother's got visitors. Perhaps we shan't be able to go down to the playroom at all.'

At eleven o'clock, when the visitors had arrived and Mother was giving them coffee and the children were handing round plates of biscuits and buns, Binky appeared at the window.

He was horrified when he saw so many people there and disappeared at once. The children caught sight of him.

They looked at one another in despair. Now what were they to do? There was only one thing. They must do something to make Mother send them out of the room.

So Mollie suddenly spilt the plate of biscuits all over the floor, and Peter spilt a cup of coffee.

Mother looked vexed. 'Oh dear – how clumsy of you!' she said. 'Go and ask Jane if she will please bring a cloth, Mollie. And I think you and Peter had better go now. I don't want anything else spilt.'

'Sorry, Mother,' said Peter.

They shot out of the room. Mollie called to Jane to take a cloth to wipe up the coffee, and then both children raced down to the playroom.

'I hope Binky hasn't gone off in the chair by himself,' panted Peter. 'If he saw us with all those visitors he might think we couldn't possibly come – and then he'd fly off alone.'

They got to the playroom door just as Binky was flying out in the Wishing-Chair. They bumped into one another, and Peter caught hold of one of the chair's legs.

'Just in time!' he cried. 'Help us up, Binky!'

Binky pulled them up with him. Then the chair flapped its green and yellow wings and flew strongly up into the air.

'I was afraid you wouldn't be able to come,' said Binky. 'I was just setting off by myself. The chair had only grown its wings a few minutes before I peeped in at the window.'

'What fine, big, strong wings it's got now,' said Peter. 'They make quite a draught round my legs. It will be able to fly faster now.'

'Where are we going?' asked Mollie.

'I don't know,' said Binky. 'I just said to the chair, "Go and find my wand, and Rosebud, and the rest of the toys," and it seemed to know the place I meant, because it rose up at once. I've no idea where we shall land. I only hope it's somewhere nice. It would be awful to go to the Village of Slipperies, or to the Land of Rubbish, or somewhere like that.'

'Oh dear – I hope it's somewhere nice too,' said Mollie. 'The chair is flying very high, isn't it?'

'Do you think it may be going to Toyland?' asked Peter. 'I wouldn't mind that at all. After all, most of the things were toys. I think it's very likely they may have gone there.'

'It certainly seems to be taking the way to Toyland as far as I remember,' said Binky, peering down. 'I know we pass over the Village of Teddy Bears before we reach

Toyland, and we're very near that now. There's Toyland, far over there. That must be where we're going.'

But it wasn't. The chair suddenly began to fly down and down at a great rate, and it was plain that it was going to land.

'Well! This isn't Toyland!' said Binky in surprise. 'Good gracious! I do believe it's the school run by Mister Grim, for Bad Brownies. Surely the toys haven't gone there!'

The chair landed in the grounds of a big house, just near a wall. Binky and the children got off. They pushed the chair under a bush to hide it. Then they looked cautiously round.

From the big building in the distance came a chanting noise. The children and Binky listened.

'I mustn't scream or whistle or shout
Because Mister Grim is always about,
I mustn't stamp or slam any door
Or jump or slide on the schoolroom floor,
I mustn't be greedy, untidy or lazy
Because Mister Grim would be driven quite
    crazy,
I mustn't be slow, and I MUST be quick,
Because Mister Grim has a very BIG STICK!'

'Ooooh!' said Mollie. 'I don't like the sound of that. That must be the poor Bad Brownie learning verses for Mister Grim.'

'Yes,' said Binky. 'I do wish we hadn't come here. I've half a mind to get in the Wishing-Chair and go off again. I've always been told that Mister Grim is a very hard master. We don't want to be caught by him.'

'*Caught!*' said Peter. 'But we're two children and a pixie – we're not brownies – and this is a school for brownies.'

'I know,' said Binky. 'I just don't like the feel of this place, that's all. If you think it's all right, we'll stay and see if we can possibly find where our toys are.'

'I think we'd better,' said Peter. 'Well – what's the first thing to do?'

'Listen – is that the brownies coming out to play?' said Mollie as a perfect babel of noise reached them. Then came the sound of feet running and in a trice about fifty small brownies surrounded them. They all looked merry, mischievous little fellows, too young to have grown their brownie beards yet.

'Who are you? Are you new pupils for this awful school?' asked a small brownie, pushing himself forward. 'My name's Winks. What's yours?'

All the little brownies crowded round, listening eagerly. Binky pushed them back.

'Don't crowd so. No, we haven't come to your school. We came because we're looking for things we've lost, and we think they may be somewhere here. My name's Binky. These are real children, Peter and Mollie.'

'Well, be careful Mister Grim doesn't see you,' said Winks. 'He's in a very bad temper these days – worse than he's ever been.'

'Why?' asked Peter.

'Because we found the cupboard where he kept his canes and we broke the whole lot!' chuckled the brownie. 'Every one of them.'

'Can't he slap you or smack you, though?' said Peter.

'Oh, yes – but we dodge,' said Winks. 'Can't dodge a cane very well, though. I say – do be careful he doesn't catch you.'

'What are you looking for?' asked another brownie. 'I'm Hoho; you can trust me.'

'Well,' said Binky, 'we came here to look for a lot of flying toys – and my new wand. It had wings too.'

'Flying toys!' said Winks. 'And a flying wand. Well! Have we seen anything like that, boys?'

'Yes!' shouted Hoho at once. 'Don't you remember? Yesterday evening we saw something very peculiar – we thought they were curious birds flying about in the air. They must have been your toys.'

'What happened to them?' asked Peter.

'Well, old Grim was out in the garden smoking his evening pipe,' said Hoho. 'And he suddenly looked up and saw them too. He was very excited, and called out some words we couldn't hear . . .'

'And what we thought were the peculiar birds came right down to him,' said Winks. 'But they must have been your toys on the way to Toyland! He caught sight of them and made them come to him!'

'Well, whatever can *he* do with them?' said Hoho. 'We are never allowed any toys at all. I suppose he will sell them to his friend the Magician Sly-Boots.'

'Oh dear,' said Mollie. 'Well, we must try and get them

before he does. Will you show us where you think Mister Grim might have hidden our toys?'

'Yes, we'll show you!' shouted the brownies. 'But do be careful you aren't caught!'

They took Binky and the children to the big building, all walking on tiptoe and shushing each other.

Hoho led them inside. He pointed to a winding stair. 'Go up there,' he whispered. 'You'll come to a little landing. On the left side is a door. That's the storeroom, where I expect Mister Grim has put the toys.'

'Creep in – and see if you can find them,' whispered Winks.

'Come on,' said Binky to the others. 'It's now or never! If we find our things we'll take them and rush down and out into the garden, and be off in the Wishing-Chair before Mister Grim even knows we're here!'

'Sh!' said Mollie, and they all began to go up the stairs on tiptoe. 'Shhhhhhh!'

CHAPTER 11

MISTER GRIM'S SCHOOL FOR BAD BROWNIES

Up the stairs went the three, treading very quietly indeed, hoping that not one of the stairs would creak or crack.

The brownies crowded round the door at the bottom of the stairs, holding their breath and watching. Up and up and up – and there was the landing at last! Now for the door on the left.

They saw the door. They tiptoed to it and Peter turned the handle. Would it be locked? No, it wasn't!

They peeped inside. Yes, it was the storeroom, and stacks of books, pencils, rulers, ink-bottles, old desks, and all kinds of things were there.

'Can't see our toys,' whispered Binky. 'Or my wand. Let's look in all the drawers and all the cupboards.'

So they began opening the drawers and hunting in them, and pulling open the cupboard doors and peering in at the shelves. But they could find nothing more exciting than books and pens and rubbers.

And then Binky gave a soft cry. 'Look here,' he said. 'Here they are!'

The others ran quickly over to him. He had opened a big chest – and there, lying quietly in the top of it, their wings vanished, lay all the toys they had lost – yes, Rosebud was there, and Peter's engine, and the top and the soldiers – everything.

But wait – no, not quite everything. 'I can't see my wand anywhere,' said Binky, hunting desperately. 'Oh, where is it?'

They hunted all through the chest, but there didn't seem to be any wand there. They looked in despair at one another. They simply *must* find Binky's wand.

'I'm glad we've found the toys,' whispered Binky, 'but it's dreadful that I can't find my wand. It's got a lot of magic in it, you know. I wouldn't want Mister Grim to use that.'

Then the children heard a noise that froze them to the floor. Footsteps – footsteps coming slowly and heavily up the stairs. Not light, quick, brownie steps, but slow, ponderous ones. Would the footsteps come to the storeroom?

In panic the children and Binky squeezed themselves into a cupboard, not having time to put away the toys they had pulled out of the chest. The door opened – and somebody walked in!

The children hardly dared to breathe and Binky almost choked. Then a voice spoke.

'SOMEONE has been here. SOMEONE has tried to steal toys. And that SOMEONE is here still. Come out!'

The children didn't move. They were much too scared to do a thing. And then poor Binky choked! He choked again, then coughed loudly.

Footsteps marched to the cupboard and the door was

flung wide open.

There stood Mister Grim – exactly like his name! He was a big, burly brownie, with a tremendous beard falling to the floor. He had pointed ears and shaggy eyebrows that almost hid his eyes.

'HO!' he said in a booming voice. 'So the SOMEONE is not one person, but three!'

Peter, Mollie and Binky came out, poor Binky still coughing. Mister Grim took them each firmly by the back of the neck and sat them down on the window-seat.

'And now will you kindly tell me why you came to steal my toys?' he said. 'How did you know they were there, and who told you about them?'

'They're not your toys, sir,' Peter said at last in rather a trembling voice. 'They're ours. We let them grow wings yesterday by using Growing Ointment on them – and they flew away. We came to fetch them.'

'A very likely story indeed,' said Mister Grim scornfully. 'And how did you come here?'

'Up the stairs,' said Mollie.

Mister Grim frowned a fierce frown. 'Don't be foolish, girl,' he said. 'I mean, how did you arrive here – by bus or train – and how did you get into the grounds?'

Binky gave the others a sharp nudge. Mollie had just been going to say that they had come in their Wishing-Chair, but she shut her mouth again tightly. Of course she mustn't give that away! Why, Mister Grim would search the grounds and find it!

'Well?' said Mister Grim. 'I am asking you a question –

and when I ask questions I expect them to be answered.'

Still no reply from any of the three. Mister Grim leaned forward. 'Shall I tell you how you came? You must have friends here among the brownies – and they helped you to climb the wall, and told you to take the toys! Aha! Don't try to say you didn't do that.'

They didn't say a word. Mister Grim got up and put the toys back in the chest. 'You,' he said to Binky, '*you* are a pixie, and I don't usually take pixies into my school. But you are a very bad pixie, I can see, and I shall keep you here. And I shall keep these two as well. I'm not sure what they are – but even if they are real, proper children, which I very much doubt, they deserve to be punished by being my pupils here for a term.'

'Oh, no!' said Mollie in horror. 'What will our mother say? You can't do that.'

'You will see,' said Mister Grim. 'Now go downstairs, find the brownie called Winks, and tell him you are to come into class when the bell rings. He will give you books and pencils and tell you where to sit.'

The three of them had to go downstairs in a row, Mister Grim behind them. They were frightened! Unless they could manage somehow to get to their Wishing-Chair, they would simply *have* to stay at Mister Grim's school!

They found Winks and told him quickly what had happened. He was very sorry. 'Bad luck!' he said. 'Very bad luck. Come on – I'll get you your books and things. Sit by me in class and I'll try and help you all I can.'

He took them into a big room and gave them books

and pencils. Almost at once a bell rang loudly and all the brownies trooped in quickly. Not one of them spoke a word. They took their places quietly and waited.

'Why were you sent here, Winks?' whispered Binky as they all waited for Mister Grim to appear.

'Because I used my grandmother's Blue Spell and turned all her pigs blue,' whispered back Winks.

'And I was sent here because I put a spell into my father's shoe-tongues and they were rude to him all the way down our street and back,' whispered Hoho.

'And I was sent because . . .' began another brownie, when slow and heavy footsteps were heard. In came Mister Grim and stood at his big desk.

'Sit!' he said, as if the brownies were all little dogs. They sat.

'We have three new pupils,' said Mister Grim. 'I regret to say that I caught them stealing – STEALING – from my storeroom. If I find out who helped them into this school and told them about the toys they came to steal, I shall take my stick to him. Brrrrrr!'

This was very frightening. Mollie didn't even dare to cry. She comforted herself by thinking of the Wishing-Chair hidden under the bush in the garden. They would run to it as soon as ever they could!

'Now we will have mental numbers,' said Mister Grim, and a little groan ran round the class. 'You, boy, what number is left when you take eighty-two and sixty-four from one hundred and three?'

He was pointing at poor Peter. Peter went red. What a silly question! You couldn't take eighty-two and sixty-four from one hundred and three.

'Say six hundred and fifty,' whispered Winks. 'He doesn't know the answer himself!'

'Six hundred and fifty,' said Peter boldly. Everyone clapped as if he were right.

'Er – very good,' said Mister Grim. Then he pointed to Mollie. 'How many pips are there in seven pounds of raspberry jam?'

'Seven pounds of raspberry jam?' repeated Mollie, wondering if she had heard aright. 'Er – well . . .'

'Say none at all, because your mother only makes raspberry jelly and strains the pips out,' whispered Winks.

'Er – none at all,' said Mollie.

'How do you make that out?' thundered Mister Grim in a very frightening voice.

'Because my mother makes raspberry jelly and strains all the pips out,' said Mollie. Everyone clapped again.

'Silence!' said Mister Grim. 'Now you, pixie – and see you are very, very careful in your answer. If I take fifty-two hairs from my beard, how many will there be left?'

Binky stared desperately at the long beard that swept down to the floor. 'Well,' he began . . . and then Winks whispered to him.

'Say "the rest"!' he hissed.

'Er – well, the rest of the hair will be left,' he said.

Mister Grim suddenly pounded on the desk with his hand. 'You, Winks!' he shouted. 'I heard you whispering then – you told him the answer – and I believe you told the others the answers too. Come here!

I'll give you the stick. Aha, you think because all my canes were broken that I haven't got one – but I have! You just wait.'

'Please, sir, I'm sorry,' said Winks. 'I just thought I'd help them as they were new. I was trying to be good, sir, and helpful, I really was. You're always telling us to be that, sir.'

'No excuses,' said Mister Grim, and he turned to a cupboard behind him. He unlocked it and took out a long, thin stick.

'Come up here, Winks,' he said, and poor Winks went up. He got two strokes on his hands. Mollie was very upset, but Hoho whispered, 'Don't worry – Winks always puts a little spell in his hands and he doesn't mind a bit if he's whacked. He doesn't feel it!'

Mollie felt comforted. Winks winked at her as he went back to his seat. Mister Grim went to take a book from a shelf – and as he turned his back Binky clutched Peter by the elbow.

'Peter,' he hissed, 'do you see what his stick is? It's my WAND!'

Peter stared. Yes – the stick on the desk was Binky's little wand. Oh, if only it had wings now and could fly to Binky!

But it hadn't. Binky never took his eyes off it as the class went on and on. 'I must get it,' he kept saying to himself. 'I MUST get it! But how can I? Oh, for a really good idea!'

CHAPTER 12
BINKY IS NAUGHTY

Morning school came to an end at last. Mister Grim rapped on his desk with his stick – Binky's wand!

'Attention, all of you!' he said. 'Dinner will be in ten minutes' time. Anyone who is late or who has dirty hands or untidy hair will go without.'

Winks groaned. 'It's awful,' he said to Peter when Mister Grim had gone out. 'There's never enough dinner for everyone, so Mister Grim just says, "Here, you, your hair is untidy," or "Here, you, your nails aren't clean," and about a dozen of us have to go without our dinner.'

'What a dreadful school!' said Peter. 'Why don't you run away?'

'How can we?' said Winks. 'You've seen the high wall round the grounds, and all the gates are locked. I wish I could get out of here; it's a horrid place, and I really would be good if I could escape.'

'Would there be room for him in the Wishing-Chair, do you think?' whispered Mollie to Binky. 'He's so nice. I'd like to help him, Binky.'

'So would I,' whispered back Binky. 'Well, we'll see.'

Poor Binky was one of those who had to go without

his dinner. Mister Grim stood at the door of the dining-hall as each brownie walked in. Every so often he pounced on one and roared at him.

'Here, you, you haven't washed behind your ears! No dinner! Here, you, why aren't your nails scrubbed? No dinner!' And when Binky tried to slip past him he hit him on the shoulder with his hand and roared: 'Here, you, why haven't you brushed your hair? No dinner!'

'I did brush it,' said Binky indignantly, 'but it's the kind of hair that won't lie down.'

'No dinner today for untidy hair, and no dinner tomorrow for answering back,' said Mister Grim.

'Oh, I say, that's not fair,' said Binky.

'And no dinner for the third day for being rude,' said Mister Grim. 'Another word from you and I'll cane you with this new stick of mine!'

He slapped the wand down so hard on a nearby table that Binky was afraid it would break in half. But fortunately it didn't.

Binky went out of the room, looking angry and sulky. Horrid Mister Grim! He joined all the brownies who were also to go without their dinner.

Peter and Mollie were very sorry for Binky. When the pudding came they tried to stuff two tarts into their pockets to take to him. But the pastry fell to pieces and their pockets were all jammy and horrid. Mister Grim saw the crumbs of pastry around their pockets as they marched past him after dinner. He tapped them with the wand.

'Aha! Trying to stuff food into your pockets. Greedy children! No dinner for you tomorrow!'

Peter tried to snatch the wand away from Mister Grim, hoping to run and give it to Binky, but Mister Grim was too quick for him. Up in the air it went, and poor Peter got a stinging slash on his arm. Fortunately his sleeve was nice and thick, so he didn't feel it much.

'Bad boy!' roared Mister Grim. 'Stay in after school this afternoon and write out one thousand times "I must not snatch".'

There was a little time before afternoon school. Peter, Binky, Mollie and Winks had a meeting in a far corner of the grounds.

'Winks, that's my wand Mister Grim has got and is

using for a stick,' said Binky.

Winks whistled. 'I *say*! That's a fine bit of news. We ought to be able to do something about that.'

'But what?' asked Binky. 'I'm so afraid he will break my wand, and then it will be no use. Somehow or other we've got to get it back.'

'Now listen,' said Winks. 'A wand will never hit its owner, you know that. Well, what about being very naughty in class this afternoon and having to go up to Mister Grim to be punished – and your wand will refuse to cane you, of course – and surely you can easily get it back then, and do a bit of magic to get yourselves free?'

'Oooh, yes,' said Binky, looking very cheerful. 'That's an awfully good idea of yours, Winks. I'd forgotten that a wand never turns against its owner. I'll be very naughty – and then we'll see what happens.'

They all went in to afternoon school feeling rather excited. What would happen? It would certainly be fun to see Binky being very naughty, to begin with – and even greater fun to see the wand refusing to punish him!

Binky began by yawning very loudly indeed. Mister Grim heard him and tapped hard on his desk with the wand – crack! crack!

'Binky? You are most impolite. Stand up during the rest of the class instead of sitting.'

Binky stood – but he stood with his back to Mister Grim.

Mister Grim glared. 'Bad pixie! You are being impolite again. Stand round the other way!'

Binky immediately stood on his hands and waved his

feet in the air. All the brownies laughed and clapped.

Mister Grim looked as black as thunder. 'Come here!' he cried, and Binky began to walk towards him on his hands. He really looked very funny indeed. Winks laughed till the tears rolled down his cheeks.

But Mister Grim didn't try to cane him that time. He told him to go and stand in the corner – the right way up.

So Binky stood in the corner the right way up, turning every now and then to grin at the others. Mister Grim began firing questions at the class. 'Hands up those who know why brownies have long beards. Hands up those who know the magic word for "disappear". Hands up those who know why green smoke always comes out of chimneys of witches' houses. Hands up . . .'

He didn't even wait for anyone to answer so the brownies just shot up their hands at each question and then put them down again and waited for the next. Peter and Mollie thought it was the silliest class they had ever attended!

'And now – can anyone ask me a question *I* can't answer?' said Mister Grim. 'Aha! It would take a clever brownie to do that! Be careful – because if I *can* answer it, you'll have to come up and be punished. Now, who will ask me a question I can't answer?'

The brownies had all been caught by this trick before, so nobody put up his hand.

Mister Grim pounced on poor Winks. 'You, brownie! Can't you think of a question?'

'Yes, sir,' said Winks at once. 'I'd like to know why gooseberries wear whiskers. Do they belong to the brownie family?'

Everybody roared at this ridiculous question. Except Mister Grim. He looked as grim as his name. He rapped with his stick on the desk.

'Come up here, Winks. I will not have you upsetting the class like this with your silly remarks.' And Winks went up, grinning. He got three strokes of the wand, but it didn't hurt him, of course, as he had still got the spell in his hands that prevented the stick from hurting him.

'I've got a question; I've got a question!' suddenly called out Binky, seeing a chance to get his wand.

'What is it?' said Mister Grim, frowning.

'Mister Grim, why do horses wear hooves instead of feet?' cried Binky.

'Come up here,' said Mister Grim sternly. 'That's another silly question.'

Binky went. 'Hold out your hand,' said Mister Grim. Binky held it out. Mister Grim brought down the wand as hard as he could – but, dear me, he missed Binky's hand altogether. The wand simply slipped to one side and didn't touch Binky's hand at all.

Mister Grim tried again – and again – and again – but each time the wand slid away from Binky's outstretched hand and hit the desk instead. It was very puzzling indeed for Mister Grim.

The brownies were all laughing. So were Peter and Mollie. Mister Grim's face was so comical to watch as he tried to hit Binky's hand and couldn't.

'I shall break this stick in two!' he cried suddenly in a rage.

That gave Binky a shock. 'No,' he shouted. 'No, you mustn't do that! You mustn't!'

'Why not?' said Mister Grim, and he put both hands on the wand as if to break it.

Peter, Mollie and Binky watched in despair, waiting for the crack.

But the wand wasn't going to let itself be broken! It slid out of Mister Grim's big hands and shot over to Binky, who caught it as it came.

'Ha!' shouted Binky in delight. 'I've got it again – my lovely wand – I've got it!'

'What! Is it a wand?' cried Mister Grim in astonishment. 'I didn't know that. Give it back to me!'

He snatched at it, but Binky was skipping down the room, waving it.

'I'll give you all a half-holiday! Yes, I will! See my wand waving to give you all a half-holiday! Go into the garden and play, all of you!'

The brownies didn't wait. They rushed out of the room at top speed, shouting and laughing. Soon only Peter, Mollie and Binky were left with Mister Grim. Winks was peeping round the door.

'How DARE you treat me like this!' shouted Mister Grim, marching towards Binky. 'I'll –'

'Go back, go back!' chanted Binky, and waved his wand at Mister Grim, whose feet at once took him six steps backwards, much to his surprise. 'You see, I've got magic in my wand,' cried the pixie. 'Aha! I may have powerful magic, Mister Grim, so be careful!'

'Come on, Binky,' whispered Peter. 'Let's go and find

the Wishing-Chair and fly off.'

'But I want my doll Rosebud before we go,' said Mollie. 'And have you forgotten your engine and all the other toys, Peter? We must take those with us. Mister Grim, give us our toys!'

'Certainly not,' said Mister Grim, and he shook a large key at them. 'See this key? It's the key of the storeroom, which I've locked. You can't get your toys and you never shall!'

'We'll see about that,' said Binky. 'We'll just see about that, Mister Grim!'

CHAPTER 13

HOME, WISHING-CHAIR, HOME!

Mister Grim stared angrily at Binky, who was still waving his wand to keep the teacher from coming any nearer to him.

'You can't get your toys, so make up your mind about that,' he said. 'And stop waving that ridiculous wand. Its magic will soon run out.'

Binky himself was a bit afraid that it would. It was a very new wand and hadn't very powerful magic in it yet. 'I think we'd better go before the wand's magic wears out,' he said in a low voice to Peter and Mollie.

They darted out of the door and Mister Grim followed. But just outside the door he ran into a crowd of brownies that popped up from nowhere quite suddenly, and over he went! When he got up the children and Binky were nowhere to be seen.

He began to run down the garden again, but once more he tripped over a mass of brownies. They weren't a bit afraid of him now because Binky had taken his stick – the wand!

Binky and the others raced to find the Wishing-Chair. Where was the bush they had hidden it in? Ah, there it was! They ran to the bush – but, oh dear, the chair wasn't there!

'One of the brownies must have found it and taken it,' said Binky. Just then Winks ran up and pulled at his arm.

'I found your Wishing-Chair and hid it in the shed,' he said. 'I was afraid Mister Grim might see it if he walked round the garden. Come along – I'll show you where it is.'

He took the three to an old broken-down shed. The roof had fallen in at one end. There were no windows to the shed, so it was very dark inside. Binky groped his way in – and immediately fell over the Wishing-Chair. He felt the legs anxiously to see if the chair still had its wings. Yes – thank goodness – it had!

The wings waved gently as they felt Binky's anxious hands. The chair creaked softly. Binky knew it was glad to have him again.

'Wishing-Chair, we must go quickly,' said Binky, and he climbed on to the seat. 'Come on, Peter and Mollie – quickly, before Mister Grim comes!'

'What about Winks? Aren't we going to take him too?' said Mollie.

'Oh – would you really?' said Winks, in delight. 'You really are very kind. I hate this school. I've been trying to escape for ages.'

He was just about to squeeze in the chair with the others when somebody appeared at the doorway. It was Mister Grim!

'So here you are!' he said, peering in. 'All complete with a Wishing-Chair too! I might have guessed that was how you came. Well, I'm going to lock this door, so you won't be able to fly out – and there are no windows at all!'

Winks leapt off the chair and ran to him. He tried to take the key from Mister Grim's hand, and the two struggled at the door.

'Fly out where the roof has fallen in, fly out there!' suddenly shouted Winks. 'The chair can just squeeze through it!'

And the chair rose up into the air and flew to where the roof had fallen in! It got stuck halfway through, but Peter broke away a bit more roof and the chair suddenly shot through and out into the open air.

'Oh, poor Winks – we've left him there,' cried Mollie, almost in tears. 'We can't leave him!'

'Go on, Chair, fly off with them!' shouted Winks from below in the shed. 'Don't mind me! Escape while you can.'

The chair flew out of hearing. Binky and Peter were very silent. Mollie wiped her eyes with her hanky. 'I think you two should have taken the chair down and tried to help Winks,' she said. 'It was wrong of you to leave him.'

'We'll go back for him,' said Binky, taking Mollie's hand. 'But, dear Mollie, you see we had *you* to think of, and both Peter and I know we have to look after you, because you're a girl. We had to think of you – didn't we, Peter?'

'Of course,' said Peter. 'You're my sister, Mollie, and you know that brothers must always look after their sisters. I couldn't possibly risk taking you down into danger again just then, when I knew Mister Grim was so angry. We'll go back for Winks, don't worry.'

'And what about our toys too?' said Mollie, with a sniff. 'I think it's very nice of you both to want to take care of me like this – but I do feel so sorry for Winks, and it's dreadful to have to leave Rosebud behind too.'

'And my engine,' said Peter, gloomily, 'and the skittles and soldiers.'

'We'll get them all back,' said Binky, comfortingly. 'You wait and see.'

The chair took them back to the playroom, flapping its wings strongly. They really were beautiful big wings. Mollie was glad they were, because now that she and Peter had grown heavier she felt that the chair really did need to be stronger.

They arrived at the playroom and flew in at the door. The chair gave a creaking sort of sigh and set itself down in its place. Its wings at once vanished.

'There! Its wings have gone already,' said Mollie, ready to cry again. 'So now we can't go and rescue Winks today.'

'Well – that's a pity,' said Binky. 'We shall just have to wait till its wings grow again. Anyway, it will give us time to make a plan for getting back our toys too. That will be difficult, you know, because if the storeroom is locked and Mister Grim keeps the key on his key-ring, and carries it about with him, I don't see at present how we can rescue the toys.'

Mother's voice was heard calling down the garden. 'Children! It's past tea-time – and you didn't come in to dinner either. Where are you?'

'Oh dear – now we shall have to go,' said Mollie. 'And we haven't planned anything. Binky, come and tell us AT

ONCE if the chair grows its wings again – and do, do try to think of a good plan.'

'Come and see me again tonight if you can,' called Binky. 'I may have a visitor here who will help us.'

Mother called again, rather impatiently. The children fled. Fortunately, Mother seemed to think they had had a picnic lunch down in the playroom, and she didn't ask any difficult questions.

'I was sorry to send you out of the room this morning,' she said. 'Especially as I expect you were not really naughty, but just nervous, and so dropped the biscuits and the coffee. Never mind – I expect you were glad not to have to stay with my visitors!'

'We were rather,' said Mollie, honestly, 'and I expect *you* were glad we kept out of your way today, Mother, really.'

'Now have your tea,' said Mother.

The children wished that Binky was with them. He had had to go without his dinner at Mister Grim's school, so he must be very hungry. Perhaps he would go out to tea with one of his pixie friends in the garden, and have a good meal.

'Now, Daddy and I are going out tonight,' said Mother, when they had finished. 'Put yourselves to bed at the right time, half an hour after your supper, and don't lie awake waiting for us, because we shall be very late.'

'Right, Mother,' said Peter, at once making up his mind to go down to the playroom after his supper, just before they went to bed. Binky's visitor might be there, and it would be fun to see him. Binky's visitors were always interesting, and sometimes very exciting.

Mother put on her lovely evening frock, and then she and Daddy said goodbye and went. The children did some jobs that Mother had asked them to do, and then found that it was supper-time. Jane brought them in bananas cut into small slices, scattered with sugar, and covered with creamy milk.

'Oooh!' said Mollie. 'This is one of my favourite suppers.'

After supper they slipped down to the playroom. Binky wasn't there. There was a note left on the table, though.

'Gone to have supper with Tickles. Felt very hungry after having no dinner. Be back later. Can you come and meet my visitor at half-past nine if you're not asleep? VERY IMPORTANT.
'Love from Binky.'

'I know, Peter,' said Mollie, 'let's go to bed now, then we can slip out for half an hour and meet Binky's visitor without feeling guilty. We simply must meet him if it's important.'

So they put themselves to bed half an hour earlier than usual.

Both children went to sleep – but Peter awoke at half-past nine because he had set the alarm clock for that time and put it under his pillow. When the alarm went off, muffled by the pillow, he awoke at once. He slipped on his dressing-gown and went to wake Mollie.

'Come on!' he whispered. 'It's half-past nine. Buck up!'

Mollie put on her dressing-gown too, and the two

of them slipped out of the garden door and down to the playroom. They peeped in at the door. Yes – Binky's visitor was there – but, dear me, what a very, very surprising one!

CHAPTER 14

MISTER CUBB'S STRANGE ARMY

Binky saw the children peeping in. He got up from the sofa and called them. 'Hallo! I'm so glad you've come. Come along in. I've got an old friend here, and I want you to meet him.'

The old friend stood up – and what do you think he was? He was a tall teddy bear, so old that his hair had turned grey! He was not as tall as they were, but a bit taller than Binky.

'This is Mister Cubbs, the ruler of Teddy Bear Village,' said Binky. The teddy bear bowed politely, and shook hands. Everyone sat down, the children and Binky on the sofa and the teddy bear in the Wishing-Chair.

'I hope you don't mind my sitting in your Wishing-Chair,' he said, politely, to the children. 'But it is really such a treat and a privilege. I have never even *seen* one before.'

'Not at all. We're very pleased,' said Peter. 'I only wish it would grow its wings, then it could take you for a short ride. It feels funny at first, but it's lovely when you get used to it.'

'I've been telling Mister Cubbs about your toys that Mister Grim has got, and won't give you back,' said Binky.

'I think Mister Grim should be forced to give them up

to you,' said Mister Cubbs earnestly. 'I propose that I raise a little army from Toyland and march on the school.'

Peter and Mollie gazed at him in wonder and astonishment. It all sounded like a dream to them – but a very exciting and interesting dream. An army from Toyland! Good gracious – whoever heard of such a thing?

'Mister Cubbs has very great influence in Toyland,' explained Binky. 'As I told you, he is head of Teddy Bear Village and very much respected and admired. In fact, he has now ruled over it for nearly a hundred years.'

'Are you really a hundred years old!' asked Mollie, amazed.

'One hundred and fifty-three, to be exact,' said Mister Cubbs, with a polite little bow. 'I became head when I was fifty-four.'

'Is it difficult to be head of Teddy Bear Village?' asked Peter.

'Well, no – not really, so long as you are very firm with the *young* teddies,' said Mister Cubbs. 'They are rather wild, you know. Now, what I suggest is this. I will send to the wooden soldiers, the clockwork animals and the sailor dolls – and also my teddies, of course, and tell them to meet me at a certain place. They will make a very fine army.'

'And you'll march on the school, I suppose?' said Binky. 'And when you have defeated Mister Grim you will rescue Rosebud, the doll, and the other toys?'

'Exactly,' said Mister Cubbs.

'Can we come too?' said Peter, excited. 'I'd simply love to see all this.'

'If only the Wishing-Chair would grow its wings when

your army is on the march, we could hover above the battle and watch,' said Mollie. 'But it never does grow its wings exactly when we want it to.'

'I'll send you word when we mean to march,' said the teddy bear. 'It will probably be tomorrow evening. Well, I must go now. Thank you for a very pleasant evening, Mister Binky.'

He shook hands with all three of them and went out of the door.

'Isn't he nice?' said Binky. 'He's a very old friend of my Great-Aunt Quick-Fingers, you know, and I've often met him at her house. I thought I'd tell him about Rosebud and the other toys, and how Mister Grim wouldn't give them back. I guessed he would help.'

The playroom clock struck ten. 'We must get back,' said Mollie, with a sigh. 'We only meant to come for half an hour. It's been lovely, Binky. I do think we're lucky, having you for a friend, and meeting all your friends and having such an interesting time.'

They went back to bed, hoping that the Wishing-Chair would grow its wings the next night if the teddy bear gathered together his curious little army.

They couldn't go down to the playroom till after tea, because Mother took them to see their granny. They raced down as soon as they could and were met by a very excited Binky.

'I'm so glad you've come. The Wishing-Chair has grown little buds of wings already – they'll sprout properly in a minute! And the teddy bear has sent to say that his army is on the march!'

'Oh – *what* a bit of luck!' cried the children, and ran to the chair. Just as they got to it the knoblike buds on its legs burst open – and out spread the lovely green and yellow wings again! They began to flap at once and made quite a wind.

'Come on,' said Peter, sitting in the chair. 'Let's go! And, Binky, don't let's forget to take Winks away from that horrid school, if we can. He can live with you here in the playroom if he hasn't got a home to go to.'

Mollie got in and Binky sat on the back of the chair. Out of the door they flew at top speed.

The Wishing-Chair was told to go to Mister Grim's. 'But *don't* go down into the grounds,' commanded Binky. 'Just hover about somewhere so that we can see what's going on, and can dart down if we need to.'

It wasn't really very long before the chair was hovering over the front gate of Mister Grim's school. Not far off were all the brownies, marching up and down in the big school yard, doing drill with Mister Grim.

Then the marching brownies suddenly caught sight of the Wishing-Chair hovering in the air, and they set up a great shout.

'Look! They've come back! Hurrah for Binky and Peter and Mollie!'

Mister Grim stared up too. He looked really furious, and, to the children's dismay, he bent down and picked up a big stone. It came whizzing through the air at them, but the Wishing-Chair did a little leap to one side and the stone passed harmlessly by.

Then Binky gave the others a nudge. 'Here comes the

army! DO look!'

The children looked – and, dear me, up the lane marched the strangest little army the children had ever imagined. First came the grey-haired teddy bear, swinging a little sword. Then came a row of wooden soldiers, beating drums. Then another row blowing trumpets. After them came a whole collection of clockwork animals.

'There's a jumping kangaroo!' cried Binky in glee. 'And a dancing bear!'

'And a running dog – and a walking elephant!' said Mollie in delight.

'And look – a pig that turns head-over-heels, and a duck that waddles!' shouted Peter, almost falling out of the chair in his excitement. 'And behind them all are the sailor dolls. Don't they look smart!'

The strange army came to the gate. The clockwork kangaroo jumped right over it to the other side. He undid the gate and opened it for the army to walk through.

The brownies saw the toys before Mister Grim did and shouted in joy. They ran to meet them. 'Who are you? Where have you come from?' they called. 'Can we play with you? We never have any toys here!'

> 'We've come for Mister Grim,
> We don't like Mister Grim,
> We've come to capture him,
> We've come for Mister Grim!'

chanted all the toys.

Mister Grim stared at them as if he couldn't believe his

eyes. 'After him!' shouted the teddy bear, and after him they went! He turned to run – but the jumping kangaroo got between his legs and tripped him up, and there he was, bumping his nose on the ground, yelling for mercy!

The toys swarmed all over him in delight.

'Don't pull my hair! Don't cut off my beautiful beard,' begged Mister Grim. The teddy bear seemed just about to saw the long beard off with his sword! The children and Binky saw it all from their seat up in the Wishing-Chair and were just as excited as the toys and the brownies.

'I'll leave you your beard on one condition,' said the teddy bear, solemnly. 'Go and get the toys you have imprisoned here and bring them out to us.'

Mister Grim got up, looking very frightened, and went indoors.

He came out with all the toys. Mollie gave a scream of delight when she saw Rosebud.

'He's even got the teapot that grew wings too,' said Peter, pleased. The chair flew down to Mister Grim, and the children took all their toys from him. Mollie cuddled Rosebud happily.

'Thank you,' she said to the grey-haired teddy bear. 'You and your army have done very, very well. Do please bring any of them to see us whenever you can.'

The brownies crowded round the chair. 'Take us back with you, take us back.'

'We've only room for one of you, and that's Winks,' said Binky, firmly. 'Come on, Winks.'

Up got Winks, grinning all over his little brownie face. The Wishing-Chair rose up in the air. 'Goodbye, goodbye!'

shouted Binky and the others. 'Let us know if Mister Grim behaves too badly to you and we'll send the army once again! Goodbye!'

Off they went, with all the toys and brownies waving madly. Mister Grim didn't wave. He looked very down in the mouth indeed – but nobody was sorry for him, not even Mollie!

CHAPTER 15

OFF TO THE LAND OF GOODIES

The summer days went on and on. The Wishing-Chair seemed to have had enough of adventures for a time, and stayed quietly in its corner, without sprouting so much as one wing.

One day Binky came tapping at the children's window. They came to it at once.

'Has the Wishing-Chair grown its wings again?' asked Peter, in excitement. Binky shook his head.

'No. I haven't come to tell you that. I've just come to show you this.'

He pushed a piece of paper into their hands. This is what it said:

'DEAR COUSIN Binky,
    'You haven't been to see my new house yet, so do come. I expect you have heard that I have moved to the Land of Goodies. It's simply lovely. Do come and see me soon. I have a biscuit tree growing in my garden, just coming into fruit, and a jelly plant growing round my front door.
'Yours ever,
'PIPKIN.'

'Well! Does your cousin *really* live there?' said Mollie, in wonder. 'How lucky you are, Binky. Now you can go and eat as many goodies as you like. I only wish we could come too.'

'I came to ask if you'd like to go with me,' said Binky. 'My cousin Pipkin won't mind. He's a very nice fellow, though I always thought he was a bit greedy. I expect that's why he bought a house in the Land of Goodies really – so that he could always have lots of things to eat. Why, if you pass a hedge you'll probably see that it's growing bars of chocolate.'

This sounded so exciting that the children felt they wanted to go at once.

'We can't,' said Binky. 'We'll have to wait for the Wishing-Chair to grow its wings again. The Land of Goodies is too far unless we go by Wishing-Chair.'

'How disappointing!' said Mollie. 'I feel awfully hungry even at the thought of going. What about Winks, Binky? Is he coming too?'

Winks had come back with them to the playroom, and had stayed a night with Binky, and then gone to tell his people that he wasn't going back to Mister Grim's again. He meant to bring back some of his things with him, and spend some of the time with Binky in the playroom and some with his other friends. He was very pleased indeed at being free.

'Winks can come if he's back in time,' said Binky. 'I don't know where he is at the moment. He's really rather naughty, you know, although he's nice, and very good fun. I hear that he met my cousin Sleep-Alone the other evening and, as soon as poor old Sleep-Alone was fast asleep in a little shed in the middle of a field, Winks took along two donkeys that had lost themselves and told them to cuddle up to Sleep-Alone.'

'Oh dear – what happened?' said Mollie.

'Well, Sleep-Alone woke up, of course, and tried to throw the donkeys out,' said Binky, 'but one of them gave him such a kick with its hind legs that he flew into the clouds, got caught on a big one, and hung there for a long time.'

'Well, it would certainly be a good place to sleep alone in,' said Mollie. 'What a monkey Winks is!'

'Yes. I'm not surprised really that his family sent him to Mister Grim's school,' said Binky. 'Well, will you come with me to the Land of Goodies, then?'

'Of *course*,' said the children. 'You needn't ask us that again.'

The next day was rainy. The children went down to the playroom as usual, but Mother made them take a big umbrella to walk under. 'It really is such a downpour,' she said.

They shook the raindrops off the umbrella as soon as they reached the playroom door. Binky's voice came to them, raised in joy. 'Is that you, Mollie and Peter? The Wishing-Chair has *just* grown its wings.'

'Oh, good!' cried Mollie, and ran in. Sure enough the chair was already waving its green and yellow wings.

'But it's pouring with rain,' said Peter, looking in at the door as he struggled to put down the big umbrella. 'We shall get soaked if we go miles through this rain.'

'We'll take the umbrella,' said Mollie. 'It will cover all three of us easily.'

'*Four* of us,' said Winks, and he popped out of the cupboard and grinned at them. 'I've come back for a day or two. I hid in the cupboard in case it was your mother or somebody coming.'

'Oh, Winks, I'm so glad you're coming too,' said Mollie. 'Can we go now, this very minute, Binky?'

'I don't see why not,' said Binky. 'Don't put down that umbrella, Peter; we'll come now and you can hold it over us as we fly.'

So very soon all four were sitting in the Wishing-Chair, flying through the rain. Peter held the big umbrella over them, and although their legs got a bit wet, the rest of them was quite dry.

'It's quite a long journey, so I hope the chair will fly fast,' said Binky. 'It will be a bit dull because the rain clouds stop us from seeing anything.'

The chair suddenly began to rise high. It went right through the purple-grey clouds, higher and higher and higher – and then at last it was through the very last of them, and the children found themselves far above the topmost clouds, full in the blazing sun!

'Well,' said Peter, trying to shut the umbrella, 'what a brainy idea of yours, Wishing-Chair. Now we shall soon be warm and dry again. Blow this umbrella! I simply *can't* shut it.'

So it had to remain open; and, as it happened, it was a very good thing it did, because Winks tried to catch a swallow going past at sixty miles an hour, and overbalanced out of the chair! He clutched at the umbrella as he fell and down he went, with the umbrella acting just like a parachute!

'Very clever of you, Winks!' said Binky, as the chair swooped down and hovered by the umbrella for Winks to climb on to the seat again. 'I hope you only do this sort of thing when there's an open umbrella to catch hold of!'

Winks looked rather pale. He sat panting on the seat. 'I got a fright,' he said. 'I really did.'

'Well, don't be frightened if you do fall,' said Mollie. 'Do what Binky did when he once fell! He changed himself into a large snowflake and fell gently to earth! He hadn't even a bruise when he changed back to himself again.'

'Very clever. I must remember that,' said Winks. 'I say, doesn't this Wishing-Chair fly fast?'

It certainly did. It flew even faster than the swallows, and passed over miles and miles of country, which lay spread out like a coloured map far below. The children caught glimpses of it through openings in the clouds.

'What's your cousin Pipkin like?' asked Mollie.

'Well, he was a bit plump,' said Binky. 'And I expect he's plumper still now that he lives in the Land of Goodies. He's very generous and kind, though he's rather greedy too. He could easily beat Mollie at eating ice-creams.'

'Could he really?' said Mollie. 'Oh, look, Binky – we're going downwards. Are we there?'

They went down and down through layers of clouds.

When they came below them they found that the rain had stopped. Binky peered down.

'Yes – we're there. Now just remember this, all of you – you can eat whatever is growing on bushes, hedges or trees, but you mustn't eat anybody's house.'

Peter and Mollie stared at him in wonder. 'Eat anybody's house! Are the houses made of eatable things, then?'

'Good gracious, yes,' said Binky. 'Everything is eatable in the Land of Goodies – even the chimneys! They are usually made of marzipan.'

The Wishing-Chair landed on the ground. The children jumped off quickly, anxious to see this wonderful land. They looked around.

Mollie's eyes grew wide. 'Look – look, Peter – there's a bush growing currant buns. It is really. And look, there's a hedge with a funny-looking fruit – it's bars of chocolate!'

'And look at that house!' cried Peter. 'It's all decorated with icing sugar – isn't it pretty? And it's got little silver balls here and there in its walls – and all down its front door too.'

'Look at these funny flowers in the grass!' cried Mollie. 'I do believe they are jam tarts! Binky, can I pick one?'

'Pick a whole bunch if you like,' said Binky. 'They're growing wild.'

Mollie picked two. 'One's got a yellow middle – it's lemon curd – and the other's got a red middle – it's raspberry jam,' she said, tasting them.

'Better come and find my cousin Pipkin,' said Binky. 'We're not supposed to come to the Land of Goodies except by invitation, so we'd better find him, so that he can say we are his guests. We don't want to be turned out before we've picked a nice bunch of jam tarts, currant buns and chocolate biscuits!'

Binky asked a passer-by where his cousin Pipkin lived. Luckily, it was very near. They hurried along till they came to a kind of bungalow. It was round and its roof was quite flat.

'Why, it's built the shape of a cake!' cried Mollie. 'And look, it's got cherries sticking out of the walls – and aren't those nuts on the roof – sticking up like they do in some cakes? Oh, Binky, I believe your cousin lives in a cakehouse!'

'Well, he won't need to do much shopping then,' said Binky, with a grin. 'He can just stay indoors and nibble at his walls!'

They went in at a gate that looked as if it were made of barley sugar. Binky knocked at the door. It was opened by a very, very fat pixie indeed! He fell on Binky in delight, almost knocked him over, and kissed him soundly on his cheek.

'Cousin Binky! You've come to see me after all!' he cried. 'And who are these nice people with you?'

'Mollie and Peter and Winks,' said Binky.

'Glad to meet you,' said Pipkin. 'Now – how would you like to see my Biscuit Tree to begin with? And after that we'll go for a nice hungry walk, and see what we can find!'

CHAPTER 16

AN AFTERNOON WITH COUSIN PIPKIN

Pipkin took them to see his Biscuit Tree. This was really marvellous. It had buds that opened out into brown biscuits – chocolate ones! There they hung on the tree, looking most delicious.

'Pick as many as you like,' said Pipkin, generously. 'It goes on flowering for months.'

'Aren't you lucky to have a Chocolate Biscuit Tree,' said Mollie, picking two or three biscuits and eating them.

'Well – it's not so good when the sun is really hot,' said Pipkin. 'The chocolate melts then, you know. It was most annoying the other afternoon. It was very hot and I sat down under my Biscuit Tree for shade – and I fell asleep. The sun melted the chocolate on the biscuits and it all dripped over me, from top to bottom. I *was* a sight when I got up!'

Everyone laughed. They ate a lot of the biscuits and then Mollie remembered something else.

'You said in your letter to Binky that you had a jelly plant,' said Mollie. 'Could we see that too?'

Pipkin led the way round to his front door. Then the children saw something they had not noticed when they had first arrived. A climbing plant trailed over the door. It had curious big, flat flowers, shaped like white plates.

'The middle of the white flowers is full of coloured jelly!' cried Mollie. 'Gracious – you want to walk about with spoons and forks hanging at your belt in this land!'

'Well, we do, usually,' said Pipkin. 'I'll get you a spoon each – then you can taste the jelly in my jelly plant.'

It was really lovely jelly. 'I should like to eat two or three,' said Mollie, 'but I do so want to leave room for something else. Can we go for a walk now, Pipkin?'

'Certainly,' said Pipkin. So off they went, each carrying a spoon. It was a most exciting walk. They picked bunches of boiled sweets growing on a hedge like grapes, they came to a stream that ran ginger beer instead of water and they actually found meat-pies growing on a bush.

The ginger beer was lovely, but as they had no glasses they had to lie down and lap like dogs. 'I should have remembered to bring one or two enamel mugs,' said Pipkin. 'We shall pass a lemonade stream soon.'

'Is any ice-cream growing anywhere?' asked Mollie longingly.

'Oh, yes,' said Pipkin. 'But you'll have to go down into the cool valley for that. It's too hot here in the sun – the ice-cream melts as soon as it comes into flower.'

'Where's the valley?' said Mollie. 'Oh – down there. I'm going there, then.'

Mollie found a sturdy-stemmed plant with flat green leaves, in the middle of which grew pink, brown or yellow buds, shaped like cornets.

'Ice-creams!' cried Mollie, and picked one. 'Oooh! This is a vanilla one. I shall pick a pink flower next and that will be strawberry.'

'I've got a chocolate ice,' said Peter.

Pipkin and Binky ate as many as the others. Binky could quite well see why his cousin had grown so fat. Anyone would, in the Land of Goodies. He felt rather fat himself!

'Now let's go to the village,' said Pipkin. 'I'm sure you'd all like to see the food in the shops there, really delicious.'

'Is there tomato soup?' asked Peter; it was his very favourite soup.

'I'll take you to the soup shop,' said Pipkin, and he did. It was a most exciting shop. It had a row of taps in it, all marked with names – such as tomato, potato, chicken, onion, pea – and you chose which you wanted to turn, and out came soup – tomato, chicken, or whatever you wanted!

'There isn't the soup *I* like best,' said Winks, sadly. 'I like pepper soup.'

'You don't!' said Binky. 'It would be terribly, terribly hot.'

'Well, I like it – and there isn't any,' said Winks.

'There's a tap over there without any name,' said Pipkin. 'It will produce whatever soup you want that isn't here.'

He took a soup-plate and went to the tap without a name. 'Pepper soup,' he said, and a stream of hot soup came out, red in colour.

'There you are, *red* pepper soup,' he said, and handed it to Winks. 'Now we'll see if it really is your favourite soup or not!'

''Course it is!' said Winks, and took a large spoonful. But, oh dear, oh dear, how he choked and how he spluttered! He had to be banged on the back, and had to be given a drink of cold water.

'It serves you right for saying what isn't true,' Mollie said to Winks. 'You didn't like pepper soup, so you shouldn't have asked for any.'

'I was just being funny,' said poor Winks.

'Well, *we* thought it was all very funny, especially when you took that spoonful,' said Peter. 'Now – can I get you a little mustard soup, Winks?'

But Winks had had enough of soups. 'Let's leave this soup shop,' he said. 'What's in the next one?'

The next one was a baker's shop. There were iced cakes of all shapes and colours set in rows upon rows. How delicious they looked!

'Wouldn't you each like to take one home with you?' said Pipkin. 'You don't have to pay for them, you know.'

That was one of the nice things about the Land of Goodies. Nobody paid anyone anything. Mollie looked at the cakes. There was a blue one there, with yellow trimmings of icing sugar. Mollie had never seen a blue cake before.

'Can I have this one, do you think?' she said.

The baker looked at her. He was as plump as Pipkin and had a little wife as plump as himself. Their dark eyes looked like currants in their round little faces.

'Yes, you can have that,' said the baker. 'What is your name, please?'

'Mollie,' said Mollie. 'Why do you want to know?'

'Well, it's to be *your* cake, isn't it?' said the baker. He dabbed the cake and suddenly in the very middle of the icing came the letters MOLLIE – Mollie! Now it really was Mollie's cake.

Peter had one with his name, and Pipkin had another. Binky chose a pretty pink cake and his name came up in white icing sugar.

Winks' name came up spelt wrongly. The letters were WINXS, and Peter pointed out that that was not the right way to spell his name. Winks hadn't noticed. He was a very bad speller. But Peter noticed it, and Winks chose another cake on which his name appeared spelt rightly.

It was all very strange indeed.

'Well, Pipkin, thank you very much for a most interesting and delicious afternoon,' said Binky, when they each had a cake to take home. 'How I'm going to eat this cake I really don't know. Actually I don't feel as if I could ever eat *any*thing again.'

They came to Pipkin's house and said goodbye to him. Then they went off to find their Wishing-Chair. Winks lagged behind, nibbling his cake. The others hurried on. They knew exactly where they had left the chair.

Suddenly they heard Binky give a loud cry of anger. 'Look! Winks is doing JUST what I said nobody was to do! He's breaking off bits of gateposts to chew – and look, he's taken a bit of window-sill – it's made of gingerbread! And now he's throwing currant buns at that marzipan chimney to try to break it off!'

So he was! Poor Winks – he simply couldn't change from a bad brownie to a good one all at once. He was tired of being good and now he was being thoroughly naughty.

Crash! Down came the chimney, and Winks ran to it to break off bits of marzipan. And round the corner came two policemen! They had heard the crash and come to see what it was. When they saw Winks they blew their whistles loudly and ran up to him.

'Well – he's really got himself into trouble again now,' said Binky. 'Isn't he silly?'

Winks was struggling hard with the two policemen. He called out to Binky. 'Save me, Binky, save me! Mollie, Peter, come and help!'

'Oho!' said the bigger policeman of the two. 'Are they your friends? We'll catch them too! No doubt they are as bad as you.'

'Quick! We must get in the Wishing-Chair and go!' said Binky. 'Winks will always get into trouble wherever he goes – but there's no need for us to as well. Where's the Wishing-Chair?'

They found it where they had left it, hidden well away under a bush. They climbed in, with Binky at the back, just as the big policeman came pounding up.

'Hey! What's all this?' he called. 'Is that chair yours?'

'YES!' shouted Binky. 'It is. Home, Chair, home. Goodbye, Winks. Say you're sorry for what you've done and maybe you'll be set free.'

Off went the chair, high into the air, leaving the big policeman gaping in surprise. He had never seen a Wishing-Chair before. They were soon out of sight.

That night, when the three of them were playing snap in the playroom, the door opened cautiously – and who should come in but Winks! The others exclaimed in surprise.

'Winks! You didn't get put into prison, then?'

'Yes,' said Winks. 'But the walls were made of chocolate cake – so I just ate my way through and got out easily. But, oh dear – I feel as if I never want to taste chocolate cake again! What is for supper?'

'CHOCOLATE CAKE,' roared everyone in delight, and Winks fled out into the night. No – he simply could not face chocolate cake again.

CHAPTER 17

A MOST ALARMING TALE

For a week Binky didn't see the children because they had gone to the seaside. They gave him all kinds of advice before they went.

'Now you see that you keep an eye on the Wishing-Chair for us, won't you?' said Peter. 'And if it grows its wings, don't you go on adventures without us. And DON'T let Winks have the chair at all. I like Winks, and he's good fun, but he's dreadfully naughty. I shouldn't be a bit surprised if he isn't sent back to Mister Grim's school again some day.'

'I know. I caught him practising magic with my wand last night,' said Binky. 'He was trying to change the teapot into a rabbit. Silly thing to do.'

'Yes, very,' said Mollie. 'You can't pour tea out of a rabbit. Now you be sure to keep an eye on Winks, Binky.'

'And don't sleep with the door or window open at night, in case the chair grows its wings when you're asleep and flies off by itself,' said Peter.

'Oh dear – it's so hot now,' said poor Binky. 'It's dreadful to have to sleep with the doors and windows shut. I've been tying the chair to my leg, so that if it does try to fly off, it will tug at my leg and wake me. Isn't that all right? I thought it was a very good idea.'

'Yes, it is,' said Peter. 'Well, so long as you remember to tie your leg and the chair's leg together at night, you can sleep with the door and windows open.'

'But watch that nobody slips in to steal the chair,' said Mollie.

Binky began to look very worried. 'I'm beginning to feel you'd better not go away,' he said. 'Anyway, don't I always look after the chair at night for you? Nothing has ever happened to it yet!'

The others laughed. 'We're being fussy, aren't we!' they said. 'Goodbye, Binky dear. A week will soon go, so don't be too lonely. I expect Winks will be popping in and out to see you.'

The children had a lovely week at the seaside and came back browner than ever. As soon as Mother would let them they rushed down to the playroom to see Binky.

He wasn't there, so they looked for a note. There wasn't one. 'Well, he's probably just gone out for a few minutes to see a friend,' said Peter. 'We'll hang up the seaweed we've brought, and tidy up the room.'

So they spent a happy ten minutes nailing up the long fronds of seaweed they had brought back, and tidying up their playroom, which seemed to have got very untidy whilst they had been away.

'It's funny Binky hasn't kept it tidier than this,' said Mollie, pulling the rugs straight, and putting a chair upright.

Then she suddenly gave a cry. '*Peter!* Where's the Wishing-Chair? It isn't here!'

Peter looked round, startled. 'Well! Fancy us not noticing that as soon as we came in! Where is it?'

'I suppose Binky's gone off in it,' said Mollie. 'He might have left a note! I suppose he's at his mother's.'

'He'll soon be back then,' said Peter, going to the door and looking out. 'He knew this was the day we were coming home.'

But Binky didn't come, and by the time tea-time came the children felt rather worried. Surely Binky would have been back to tea on the day they came home? He always liked to spend every minute with them that he could, especially now that they had to go to boarding school and leave him for months at a time.

They had brought their tea down to the playroom. They were sitting having it, rather solemnly, when a small mischievous face looked round the door. It was Winks.

'Hallo!' he said, but he didn't smile. He looked very grave and walked in quietly.

'Where's Binky?' asked Mollie at once.

'And where's the Wishing-Chair?' said Peter.

'An awful thing happened two nights ago,' said Winks. 'I hardly like to tell you.'

This was most alarming. The children stared at Winks in dismay. 'For goodness' sake tell us,' said Mollie.

'Well,' said Winks, 'I was staying here with Binky that night. I was to sleep on that rug on the floor with a cushion, and Binky was to sleep on the sofa as usual. When we were tired we got ready for bed.'

'Go on,' said Peter, impatiently. 'I want to know what's happened to Binky.'

'I went to sleep,' said Winks, 'and I suppose Binky did too. I suddenly woke up to hear a terrible noise going on – Binky shouting and yelling, and furniture being upset and goodness knows what. I put on the light, and what do you think had happened? Why, you know Binky always ties a rope from the chair to his foot, don't you – well, the chair grew its wings that night and we didn't wake – so it tried to fly out of the door all by itself, and –'

'The rope pulled on Binky's foot and woke him!' said Peter.

'Yes, the chair pulled him right off the sofa,' said Winks. 'He must have landed with an awful bump on the floor, and I suppose he thought someone had pulled him off and there was an enemy attacking him – so he was fighting the furniture and the rugs and shouting and yelling – and all the time the chair was tugging at his foot, trying to fly off!'

'Gracious!' said Mollie. 'What happened in the end?'

'Well, when I put the light on I saw the chair struggling to get out of the door, and it was dragging Binky along,' said Winks. 'I ran to stop the chair, but it rose into the air, dragged poor Binky out into the garden, and flew up into the sky!'

'What about Binky?' asked Mollie in a trembling voice.

'Oh, Mollie – poor, poor Binky had to go too, hanging upside down by one foot,' said Winks blinking away tears. 'I couldn't do anything about it, though I did try to catch hold of Binky. But he was too high up by that time.'

'This is awful,' said Mollie. 'Whatever are we to do? Has the chair gone to his mother's, do you think?'

'No. I thought of that,' said Winks. 'I went next day to see, but Binky's mother said she hadn't seen either Binky *or* the chair. She's very worried.'

'But *why* didn't the chair go to Binky's mother?' wondered Peter. 'Binky would have been sure to yell out to it to go there.'

'Well, I think the chair was frightened,' said Winks. 'It didn't know it had got Binky by the foot, you see. It couldn't understand all the yelling and struggling. It just shot off into the night, terrified.'

'This is awfully bad news,' said Mollie. 'Both Binky *and* the chair gone. And we don't know where. How can we find out?'

'I don't know,' said Winks, who looked very tired. 'I've been all over the place, asking and asking.'

'Poor Winks,' said Mollie. 'You do look very tired. I suppose you've been worried to death about Binky.'

'Yes, I have,' said Winks. 'You see, I've been teasing him rather a lot – and I hid his wand and made him cross – and I broke a cup – and now I feel awfully sorry I was such a nuisance to him.'

'You're really not very good at times, Winks,' said Peter, sternly. 'You ought to be careful, in case you get sent back to Mister Grim.'

'Yes, I know,' said Winks.

'The awful part is, even when we do find out, if ever we do, we haven't got the Wishing-Chair to fly off in to rescue him,' said Peter, gloomily.

'Shall we go and ask Mr Spells if he can help us?'

said Mollie, suddenly. 'He's awfully clever. He might think of some way of finding out where Binky's gone.'

'Yes – that's a very good idea,' said Peter. 'You've heard about Mr Spells, haven't you, Winks? Shall we go straight away now? I think I remember the way. We have to go to the Village of Pin first, and then take the bus, and then a boat.'

'Yes,' said Winks, cheering up. 'I feel much better since I've talked to you.'

They set off. Down the garden they went, and through the gap in the hedge. Into the field, and across to find the dark patch of grass. It was still there. They all sat down in it and Mollie felt about for the little knob that set the magic going.

She found it and pressed it. Down shot the ring of grass, much too fast, and they all tumbled off in a heap below. 'Gracious!' said Winks. 'You might have warned me what was going to happen. I nearly died of fright when the earth fell away beneath me!'

'Come on,' said Peter. 'We have to go down this passage now – past all these doors. We really *must* find Mr Spells as soon as possible.'

They went on down the twisting passage, which was still lighted clearly by some light nobody could see. Winks wanted to stop and read the names on each door.

'"Dame Handy-Pandy",' he said. 'Whoever is she? And this name says "Mr. Piggle-Pie." Oh, let's knock and see what he's like.'

'Winks! Come along at once,' said Mollie. 'We're in a hurry!'

124

'Wait!' cried Winks. 'Look at this door! Look at the name. Hey, Mollie. Peter – it says "MRS SPELLS!" Do you think she's anything to do with *Mr* Spells? Let's find out.'

And he banged hard at the little green door. 'RATTA-TATTA-TAT!' Oh, Winks – now what have you done?

CHAPTER 18

MR SPELLS' MOTHER

RATTA-TATTA-TAT!

The echo of Winks' knocking at Mrs Spells' door filled the underground passage and made the children jump. They turned round angrily.

'Winks! You shouldn't do that!'

'But I tell you, it says "*MRS* Spells" on this nameplate,' began Winks. Just then the door opened and a black cat stood politely there, with a little apron round its tubby waist.

'If you've brought the papers, please don't knock so loudly again,' said the cat, politely but crossly. 'We were in the middle of a spell, and you made my mistress upset half of it. Now we've made a spell to make things small instead of big. It's most annoying.' He slammed the door, almost hitting Winks' nose. The children came running up, Peter calling out breathlessly:

'I say! I do believe that was old Cinders, Mr Spells' cat! He had such enormous green eyes – like green traffic lights shining out!'

'Was it really?' said Mollie. 'Well, let's ask him if he is. Why, Mr Spells might be here himself! It would save us quite a long journey.'

'Dare we knock again?' said Peter. 'That cat was really very cross.'

'I'm not afraid of a cross cat!' said Winks boldly, and he lifted the knocker and knocked again. He also found a bell and rang that too.

'RATTA-TATTA-TAT! JINGLE-JANGLE-JING!'

Mr Piggle-Pie's door flew open and a cross voice called, 'Who's making that row? Just wait till I get dressed and I'll come and chase you!'

'That must have been Mr Piggle-Pie,' said Winks. 'Bother! He's shut his door again. Now I shan't know what he's like!'

Then Mrs Spells' door flew open, and the cat appeared again. But this time it behaved much more like a real cat. It spat at Winks and scratched him on the hand.

It was just about to shut the door again when Peter called out, 'I say, aren't you Cinders?'

The cat stared at him. 'Yes, I'm Cinders. Oh, I remember you. You're the boy who came with a girl to rescue Binky – and I helped my master do a spell to wake him up. What are you doing here, hammering at our door?'

'Well, we were really on our way to see Mr Spells,' said Peter. 'But Winks here noticed the name "Mrs Spells" on the door, and he knocked. He thought she might be some relation to Mr Spells.'

'She is. She's his mother,' said Cinders. 'I came here to help the old lady with a new spell – the one you spoilt by making her jump. My master is coming to call for me in a few minutes.'

127

'Oh, *is* he?' cried Peter joyfully. 'Then do you think we might stay and see him – we do so badly want his help.'

'Well, come in, then,' said the cat. 'I don't know about this brownie though – Winks, do you call him? Banging and ringing like that. You wait till Mr Piggle-Pie is dressed and comes after him. He'll get such a spanking.'

'I don't want to stay out in the passage,' said Winks, nervously. 'I'll be very good and quiet and helpful if you'll let me come in.'

'Who is it standing gossiping at the door?' suddenly called an annoyed voice. 'Tell them either to go or to come in.'

'You'd better come in and wait for Mr Spells,' said Cinders. So they all trooped in and Cinders shut the door. Winks was quite glad to be out of the passage, away from a possibly furious Mr Piggle-Pie.

The cat led them into a remarkably big room, with three windows. The children were so astonished to see what the windows looked out on that they quite forgot their manners for the moment, and didn't greet the bent old lady who sat in a chair in the middle of the room.

One window looked out on the sea! Yes, the sea, as blue as could be! Another looked out on a sunny hillside. The third looked out on an ordinary backyard, where washing was blowing in the wind. Most extraordinary.

'Well!' said rather a peevish voice, 'have the children of today no manners at all? Can't you even say how do you do to an old lady?'

'Oh dear,' said Mollie, ashamed of herself. 'Please, Mrs

Spells, I'm so sorry – do forgive us – but it did seem so extraordinary seeing three windows like this – in an underground room – and one looking out on the sea too. Why, I thought the sea was miles and miles away!'

'Things aren't always what they seem,' said Mrs Spells. 'What is miles away for you, may be quite near for me. Now, what was all this noise about at my front door? When I was younger I would have turned you all into pattering mice and given you to Cinders, for making a noise of that sort in a respectable place like this!'

'Madam,' said the cat, seeing that the old lady was working herself up into a temper, 'Madam, these children know Mr Spells, your son.'

The old lady beamed at once. 'Oh, do you know my son? Why didn't you tell me that at once? Cinders, some strawberryade, please, with strawberry ice, and some strawberry biscuits.'

This sounded exciting – and when it came, beautifully arranged on a large silver tray by Cinders, it was just as exciting as it sounded!

It was a pink drink made of strawberry juice. In it were pieces of ice shaped like strawberries, and the biscuit had tiny sugar strawberries in the middle!

'This is lovely,' said Peter. 'Thank you very much.'

There came the sound of a key in the door. 'Ah – my son, Mr Spells!' said Mrs Spells. 'Here he is!'

And there he was again, just the same as before, tall and commanding, but this time dressed in a long green cloak that shimmered like water. He looked very surprised indeed to see the visitors.

'Why – I've seen you before!' he said to the children. 'How are you? Quite well, I hope. And let me see – have I seen this brownie before? Yes – I have. Aren't you the bad fellow who turned all his grandmother's pigs blue? Isn't your name Winks?'

'Yes, Mr Spells, sir,' said Winks.

'I hope you got spanked for that,' said Mr Spells. 'I had a terrible job turning the pigs back to their right colour again. I believe they've still got blue tails.'

Winks wished the floor would open and swallow him up, but it didn't. Mr Spells turned to Peter.

'Well, have you come visiting my dear old mother?' he said.

Peter explained how it was they were in his mother's room. Then he told the enchanter about poor Binky and the chair.

'Good gracious!' said Mr Spells. 'We must certainly find out where that chair has gone. If it falls into the hands of some rogue he can use it for all kinds of wrong purposes. And Binky too – what a silly thing to do, to tie his foot to the chair! Why didn't he tie the chair to the doorhandle, or something like that?'

'We didn't think of that,' said Peter. 'Can you help us to find out where the chair is, and Binky too, Mr Spells?'

'Of course,' said Mr Spells. 'Now, let me think for a moment. This happened at night, you say – and the chair, as usual, flew up into the sky?'

'Yes,' said everyone.

'Well, then – who was about that night in the sky,

who might possibly have seen the chair and Binky?' said Mr Spells thoughtfully.

'Hoot, the owl,' said the old lady at once.

'Quite right, Mother,' said Mr Spells. 'Splendid idea. We'll call Hoot, the owl, and see if he knows anything about this. He's a very wise and observant bird, you know,' he said, turning to the children. 'Never misses anything that goes on at night.'

'Shall we go and ask him if he knows anything then?' said Mollie. 'Where does he live?'

'Oh, we'll get him here,' said Mr Spells 'That's the easiest way. I'll go and call him.'

He went to the window that looked out on the sunny hillside. He clapped his hands three times and muttered a word so magic that Winks trembled in his shoes. And a very curious thing happened. The sunny hillside went dark – as dark as night – and behind the trees shone a little moon! It was all very peculiar, especially as the sun still shone out in the backyard and on the sea that could be seen from the other windows!

'I must make it dark, or the owl won't come,' explained Mr Spells. 'Now I'll call him.'

He put his hands up to his mouth, placed his thumbs carefully together, and blew gently – and to the children's delight and surprise, the hoot of an owl came from his closed hands. 'Ooo-ooooooo-oooh! Ooo-ooo-ooh!'

An answering hoot came from outside the window. A dark shadow passed across the room. Then a big owl flew silently down and perched on Mr Spells' shoulder.

He caressed the big-eyed creature, whilst Cinders looked on rather jealously.

'Hoot,' said Mr Spells. 'Listen carefully. Two nights ago a Wishing-Chair flew off into the sky, and hanging to it by a rope tied to his foot was a pixie called Binky. Did you see anything of this?'

'Ooooooo-ooo-ooo! Oooooo-oo! Ooooh! Ooooo-oo-oo-oo-oo-oo-oo-oo-ooooooooh!' answered the owl, hooting softly into Mr Spells' ear.

'Thank you, Hoot,' said Mr Spells, looking grave. 'You may go.'

The owl flew off silently. Mr Spells waited a moment and then muttered another magic word. The moonlit hillside grew lighter and lighter – and, hey presto! it was the sun behind the trees now and not the moon – daylight was everywhere!

'What did the owl tell you?' asked Peter.

'Oh – I forgot you couldn't understand,' said Mr Spells. 'Well, he saw the chair – and Binky too, dangling by his foot. He followed them out of curiosity – and he says they flew near the Wandering Castle, where Giant Twisty lives, and the giant must have seen them and captured them. He saw no more of them after that.'

This was very bad news indeed. 'Oh dear – whatever are we going to do, then?' said Peter at last. 'Poor little Binky!'

'I must help you,' said Mr Spells. 'I can't let Twisty own that chair. Sit down. We must think of a plan!'

CHAPTER 19

AWAY ON ANOTHER ADVENTURE

'We can't do anything this evening,' said Mr Spells. 'That's quite certain. Anyway, the first thing to do is to find out where the Wandering Castle is.'

'Don't you know?' said Mollie, in surprise, as she thought Mr Spells knew everything.

'I know where it was last year, and the year before, and even last month,' said Mr Spells, 'but I don't know where it is now. It may have wandered anywhere.'

'Oh – does it move about?' asked Peter in amazement.

'Good gracious, yes! It's always wandering,' said the enchanter. 'One day it may be here, the next it's somewhere else. Giant Twisty finds that very useful because he's always getting into trouble because of his bad ways, and it's very convenient to have a castle that can slip away in the night.'

'It's going to be very difficult to find, isn't it?' said Mollie. 'I mean, even if we find out where it is now, it may not be there when we get there.'

'True. But there's a chance it may rest in the same place for some weeks,' said Mr Spells. '*Winks,* what are you doing?'

Winks jumped. 'Just – just stirring this stuff in the pot,' he said.

'Look at your hands!' thundered Mr Spells. 'You've been dipping them in – and now see what you've done! Meddlesome little brownie!'

Winks looked at his hands. Oh dear, they were bright blue! He stared at them in horror.

'Now you know what your grandmother's pigs must have felt like when you turned them blue,' said the enchanter. 'Well, keep your blue hands. Every time you look at them you can say to yourself, "I must not meddle. I must not meddle".

Winks put his hands into his pockets, looking very doleful.

'Well, children,' said Mr Spells, 'I think you'd better leave things to me tonight. I'll do my best to find out where the Wandering Castle happens to be at the moment and we will make a good plan to get back the chair and Binky. Can you come along early tomorrow morning?'

'Yes. We'll ask Mother to let us go out for the day,' said Peter. 'Come on, Mollie. Thank you, Mr Spells, for your help. Goodbye, Mrs Spells. Goodbye, Cinders.'

'You can go out of this door if you like,' said the enchanter, and the children suddenly saw a small silver door gleaming in the wall near the window that looked out on the hillside. They were sure it hadn't been there before. Cinders opened it for them.

He bowed politely to the children, but dug a claw into Winks, who yelled and shot outside in a hurry. Winks shook a bright blue fist at the cat.

'Where are we?' said Peter, as they walked down the hillside, now filling with shadows as the sun sank low. 'Goodness – why, there's our garden!'

So it was, just nearby. How very extraordinary. 'If only people knew how near their gardens are to curious and wonderful places, how surprised they would be!' said Mollie, walking in at their side-gate, and going to the playroom. 'Well, we can take that short cut tomorrow. I do wonder how it is that the sea is outside that other window. I just simply can't understand that!'

They said goodbye to Winks, who had tried in vain to wash the blue off his hands under the garden tap. Then off they went to ask their mother if they could have the whole day to themselves tomorrow. She said, Yes, of course they could! It would do them good to go into the country in the lovely summer weather they were having now.

'Well, I don't know what Mother would say if she knew we were going to hunt for Giant Twisty in his Wandering Castle!' said Peter. 'I suppose she just wouldn't believe it.'

The next day the children had breakfast very early indeed, and then set off down the garden to collect Winks. His hands were still as blue as ever, so he had put on a pair of gloves.

'Oh – you've borrowed them from my biggest doll, Winks,' said Mollie. 'You might have asked permission first. I should have said, "No, certainly you can't have them".'

'Yes. I felt sure you wouldn't let me,' said Winks. 'That's why I didn't ask you. I'll take great care of them, Mollie,

I really will. Your doll doesn't mind a bit.'

They went out of the garden gate and looked round. Where was that short cut now? They couldn't find it at all! But Winks spotted it.

'I've better eyes for strange things than you have,' he said. 'I can see a little shining path in the grass that you can't see. Follow me.'

'Well, you must be right,' said Peter, as Winks led them straight over the grass to the same trees on the same sunny hillside as they had seen the day before. 'And there's the little silver door!'

Cinders opened it as they came near. Winks shot in so quickly that he hadn't time to scratch the brownie, though he did try!

Mr Spells was there, surrounded by papers and old books of all kinds. 'My mother is still asleep in bed,' he said. 'I'm glad you're early. We can start off straight away.'

'Oh – have you found out where the Wandering Castle is?' asked Mollie, in delight. 'Did your magic books tell you?'

'They helped,' said Mr Spells. 'And Cinders and I did a little Find-Out Spell we know. Wandering Castle is now on the island belonging to Giant Small-One, Twisty's brother.'

'Giant Small-One – that's a funny name,' said Mollie.

'Not really,' said Mr Spells. 'He's small for a giant, that's all. Well, we'd better start!'

'But how can we get to an island?' said Peter. 'We haven't a Wishing-Chair to fly over the sea!'

'That doesn't matter,' said Mr Spells. 'Cinders has

been getting my ship ready.'

He pointed to the window that so surprisingly looked out on the sea. The children stared in wonder and delight. A most beautiful ship rocked gently on the calm blue sea, a picture of loveliness with its big, white sails. Mollie cried out in joy. 'Oh – what a beauty! And it's called *The Mollie!*'

'Just a little compliment to you,' said Mr Spells, smiling. 'Also it's supposed to be lucky to sail in a ship bearing one of the passengers' names. Well – shall we set off? The wind is just right.'

Cinders opened the window. Just outside was a stone ledge, with steps leading down to a tiny jetty. Cinders went first and helped Mollie down.

They all stepped aboard the beautiful white sailed ship. Mr Spells took the tiller.

> 'Blow, wind, blow.
> And on we will go
> Over the waters blue,'

he sang, and the white ship leapt forward like a bird.

'Is that a spell you sang?' said Mollie.

'Oh, no – just a little song,' said Mr Spells. And he began to sing again, whilst the ship sailed lightly over the blue waters. The children and Winks enjoyed it very much. Mollie trailed her hand in the water.

'Did we bring any food?' asked Mollie, suddenly. 'I'm hungry!'

'No,' said Mr Spells, and everyone at once looked rather gloomy. 'Enchanters don't need to,' he went on.

'I always carry a spell in my pocket that I use when I need any food.'

Soon they were all eating and drinking, as the ship sped on and on.

For two hours the ship sailed on – then Cinders gave a shout. 'Land ahoy! It's the island, Mr Spells, sir.'

'Aha!' said the enchanter. 'Now we must be a bit careful.' They all looked hard at the island that was rapidly coming nearer as the ship sped over the water. It didn't look very big. It was crowded with tall buildings, some of them looking like palaces, some like castles.

'Which is the Wandering Castle, I wonder?' said Mollie.

'Can't possibly tell,' said Mr Spells. 'Now here we go towards this little jetty. We'll land there. You'll have to watch out a bit, because several giants live here and you don't want to be trodden on like ants.'

Mollie didn't like the sound of this much. She was determined to keep very close to Mr Spells. Cinders was left with the ship, much to Winks' relief. They all set off up an extremely wide street.

'We shall be all right if we keep to the narrow pavements that run beside the walls of the building,' said Mr Spells, guiding them to one. 'There are plenty of small folk living here, as well as giants.'

So there were – pixies and brownies and goblins and elves – but there were also giants, and Mollie suddenly saw a most enormous foot, followed by another one, walking down the street! She shrank close to Mr Spells.

When the giant came by the children tried to see up

to the top of him, but he was too tall. 'That's a large-sized giant,' said Mr Spells. 'I know him – nice fellow called Too-Big. Here's a smaller one.'

It was exciting and extraordinary to see giants walking about. Mr Spells guided them to a palace not quite so tall as some of the buildings.

'This is where Giant Small-One lives – the giant the island belongs to,' he said. 'Come along – we will ask him whereabouts his brother's Wandering Castle is. Don't be afraid. I am much more powerful than he is and he knows it.'

They went up a long, long flight of steps. At the top was a big open door, leading into a vast hall. At the end of the hall sat a giant – but he was such a small one that he wasn't more than twice the size of the enchanter himself!

'Advance, Mr Spells, and pay your respects to Giant Small-One,' boomed an enormous voice from somewhere.

And Mr Spells boldly went forward. Now to find out what they all wanted to know!

CHAPTER 20

WANDERING CASTLE AT LAST

Mr Spells made a small bow. 'Greetings, Giant Small-One,' he said. 'I see you have not yet found a spell to make you Tall-One instead of Small-One. I come to ask you a question. We want to find your brother, Giant Twisty. Is Wandering Castle on your island?'

'I believe so,' said the voice of Giant Small-One, rather a feeble voice for a giant. 'Go to High Hill and you will see it there. Why does Mr Spells, grand enchanter, want my brother?'

'That is my own business,' said Mr Spells. The children thought he was very bold indeed to speak to a giant like that.

'Pray stay to a meal,' said Small-One, and he clapped his big hands, making a noise like guns cracking. 'I have few guests as important as you.'

'Thank you, no,' said Mr Spells. 'Our business is urgent. We will go.'

He walked back to the children and Winks, and they made their way to the door. But it was shut! They couldn't open such a big door themselves, so they had to go all the way back to Small-One and ask for a servant to open the door.

It took a long time to find a servant, which was strange, considering how many there had been in the hall a few minutes before. 'He is delaying us,' said Mr Spells angrily. 'He wants to get a message to his brother, before we reach him, to warn him that we are on his track!'

At last a servant was found, the door was opened and they all trooped down the endless steps. They made their way down the street, came into a wide lane, lined with hedges as high as trees, and then found a signpost that said 'To High Hill'.

'There's High Hill,' said Peter, pointing across the fields to a very tall hill. 'There are quite a lot of buildings on it. I wonder which is Wandering Castle?'

They came to High Hill at last and toiled up it. They met a small pixie running down, and Mr Spells hailed her.

'Hey, little pixie! Where's Wandering Castle?'

'Let me see, now – I saw it yesterday,' said the little pixie. 'Yes, I remember now. It's in the Silver Buttercup Field, sir.'

'*Silver* Buttercups!' said Mollie, astonished. 'I've never heard of those. I don't think I should like them. The golden ones are just right.'

'I agree with you,' said Mr Spells, guiding them round a big house. 'But some enchanters are very silly – always trying out novelties, you know. Well, here we are – here is Silver Buttercup Field.'

So it was. Silvery buttercups nodded in a great shimmering carpet. 'Beautiful, but washed-out looking,' said Mr Spells. 'The thing is – where's Wandering Castle? It's certainly not here! It's wandered away again. Small-One got a message to his brother in time – whilst we were trying to get that door open. Well, where has it wandered to now?'

'Please, sir, I know!' said a small goblin, running up. 'It's gone to Loneliness! I don't know if you know that country, sir. It's over the sea to the east – a very, very lonely place, where nobody ever goes if they can help it. It is going to hide itself there till you've given up looking for Twisty and his castle.'

'How do you know all this?' demanded Mr Spells.

'Because I was lying resting in these buttercups when a servant from Giant Small-One came running up to warn Twisty that you were after him,' said the goblin. 'And I heard Twisty say where he was going.'

'Right. Thank you very much,' said Mr Spells. 'Come along, children – back to the ship. We must sail off to Loneliness at once. Twisty could easily hide himself in that strange, desolate land without anyone finding him for years.'

'Oh dear – we really must find him, because of Binky,' said Mollie. They went back to the ship. Cinders was so pleased to see them back so soon that he quite forgot to try and scratch Winks as he got on board.

They set off again, the wind filling the sails and making the ship fly like a bird. She rocked up and down lightly as she went, and the children began to feel very sleepy.

They fell asleep. Mr Spells awoke them after a time. 'Mollie! Peter! We're here. Wake up, both of you.'

They sat up in the ship. It was moored to a small

pier. Mollie looked out on the land of Loneliness. It was a gloomy, desolate place, with enormous trees growing in thick masses. 'There are forests and forests of those,' said Mr Spells, looking as gloomy as Loneliness looked. 'How we shall ever know where the Wandering Castle is, I can't imagine!'

They landed, and walked towards the nearest forest of trees. Just as they got there they heard a voice shouting furiously.

'No peace anywhere! None at all! I come here, where nobody ever goes – and what comes walking almost on top of me but a castle! A CASTLE! Just when I thought I was going to sleep alone in peace!'

And out of the trees burst Binky's cousin, Sleep-Alone! He was just as surprised to see the children and Winks and Mr Spells as they were to see him.

'Sleep-Alone! Oh, Sleep-Alone, you're just about the *only* person who would come here!' cried Peter. 'Where is that castle you've been complaining about? It's Giant Twisty's, and he's got Binky a prisoner there.'

'Good thing too,' grumbled Sleep-Alone. 'Mischievous creature, always coming and disturbing me at night!'

'Listen, Sleep-Alone,' said Mr Spells. 'If you will lead us to that castle, we plan to rescue Binky and the Wishing-Chair – and we will turn the wicked Twisty out of his castle. Then it will be empty, in the middle of the land of Loneliness. And *you* shall have it for your own! Think of being alone there, with no one to wake you at night, no one to bother your!'

Sleep-Alone listened to all this in delight. What, have a large empty castle all to himself, with a thousand rooms to sleep in – lost in the middle of a forest in the land of Loneliness? Wonderful!

'I'll show you where it is,' he said eagerly.

They followed him. He darted in and out of the trees, following no path that they could see – and then at last they saw Wandering Castle! It stood there, rocking a little in the wind, for it had no true foundations as other buildings have. It was tall and dark and gloomy – and it hadn't a single window of any kind!

'There you are!' said Sleep-Alone. 'A very fine castle too – only one door – and no windows. Just the place for me!'

Mr Spells looked at the castle in silence. One door – and no windows. A very difficult place to escape from if they got inside. But they must get inside. There was no doubt about that.

'Stay here by the door, Sleep-Alone,' said Mr Spells at last. 'We're going in.' He went up the broad steps to the great studded door.

The door opened. A giant stood there, a cross-eyed fellow, with a twisted smile on his face.

'Come in,' he said. 'So you've found me, have you? Well, I'm not going to deny that I've got the Wishing-Chair – yes, and Binky too – and now I'll have you as well.'

To the children's surprise, Mr Spells didn't run away. He stepped inside and the children and Winks went too, all feeling rather scared. Twisty laughed.

'This is easier than I thought!' he said. 'How are you going to get out again, Mr Spells? There is now no door – and, as I dare say you have seen, there are no windows at all!'

The children turned and looked behind them. The door had vanished. They were indeed prisoners. But Mr Spells didn't seem at all disturbed.

'Where is Binky?' he said.

'Follow me,' said Twisty, and he went down a long dark passage and through a door. He crossed the room beyond the door, and came to another one. The door to this was locked and bolted. He opened it.

Inside was Binky, sitting miserably in the Wishing-Chair! He leapt up in the greatest joy when he saw the others. Mollie ran to him and flung her arms round him.

'Binky! You're safe! Oh, Binky, we've come to rescue you!'

Peter slapped Binky on the back and Winks pumped his hand up and down, yelling, 'Binky, good old Binky!'

In the middle of all this there came the sound of the door being slammed and bolted. Then they heard Twisty laughing loudly.

'Easy! Too easy for words! You can't get out, Mr Spells, however powerful you are. This door has a Keep-Shut Spell in it that I bought from an old witch years ago. And it's the only way out! You can go free if you give me some spells I've wanted for years.'

'You'll never get them from me, Twisty,' called Mr Spells. 'Never!'

'Mr Spells! You *are* going to get us out of here, aren't you?' begged Mollie.

'Sh! Don't get alarmed,' said Mr Spells. 'I am going to do a spell on us all. Yes, and on the Wishing-Chair too. Now, where's my chalk?'

He found a white chalk in his pocket and a blue one too. He drew first a white circle and then a blue one inside it. He made the children, Binky and Winks sit down in the middle of it.

Then he got inside the circle himself, and sat down in the Wishing-Chair.

'I'm going to say very magic words,' he said. 'Shut your eyes, please – and don't be surprised at whatever happens!'

CHAPTER 21
A VERY EXCITING TIME

The children, Binky and Winks shut their eyes. Mr Spells began to mutter some magic words under his breath – then he spoke some aloud and then he suddenly shouted three spell-words at the top of his voice, making everyone jump violently.

There was a silence. Then Mr Spells spoke in his ordinary voice. 'You can open your eyes now. The spell is done.'

They opened their eyes and looked round them in wonder. They were in the very biggest room they had ever seen in their lives. The floor stretched endlessly away from them. The walls seemed miles away. Not far from them was a colossal wooden pillar – or what looked like one. The ceiling seemed to have disappeared or else was so far away that they couldn't see it. Certainly there was no sky above them, so probably the ceiling was still there!

'What's that enormous wooden post?' said Peter in wonder. 'It wasn't here just now.'

'It's the leg of the table,' said Mr Spells surprisingly.

'What do you mean?' said Peter. 'It's much too big for that – look, that's the wooden pillar I mean – over there. And where are the chalk circles gone?'

'We're still standing in the middle of them,' said Mr Spells with a laugh. 'Do you mean to say you don't know what has happened?'

'No,' said Peter. 'I feel funny, you know – but except that we appear to be in quite a different place now I don't know what's happened.'

'*I* do,' said Binky. 'You've used a very powerful Go-Small Spell, Mr Spells, haven't you? Goodness, I was awfully afraid you weren't going to stop the spell soon enough – I thought we were going to shrink to nothing. How big are we?'

'Smaller than mice,' said Mr Spells. 'I wanted to make us small enough to creep under the door, you see.'

'How clever of you!' said Mollie joyfully. 'I see what has happened now – why the ceiling seems so far away, and why that table-leg looks like a great pillar – and why we can't see the chalk circles – we'd have to walk a long way to get to them now!'

'Quite right,' said Mr Spells. 'Now I think we'd better make a move, in case the giant comes back and guesses what I've done. I'm glad the spell went so well – sometimes a powerful spell like that makes loud noises, and I've known it to make lightning come round the circle.'

'Gracious!' said Peter. 'I wish it had. I'd have enjoyed our own private little storm!'

'Now the thing is – where's the door gone?' said Binky. 'We've gone so small that the room is simply enormous, and the wall where the door is seems miles away. We'd better begin walking right round the walls till we come to the door!'

But Mr Spells knew where the door was. Carrying the Wishing-Chair, which had gone small too, he led them for what seemed miles over the floor, and they at last came to where the door was fitted into the wall. A draught blew at them as they came near to the enormous door.

'That's the draught blowing under the bottom of the door,' explained Mr Spells. 'Now – I'm going to squeeze under first to see that everything is safe. Be ready to follow me when you hear me call.'

He disappeared under the door, bending himself double. Soon they heard his voice. 'Yes – come along – it's all right.'

One by one they squeezed under the door, and found themselves in what they supposed must be the room outside – but now, of course, it seemed a very vast dark place indeed. 'Shall I make us our right size again – or shall I keep us small?' wondered Mr Spells. 'On the whole, I think I'll keep us small.'

He led them across the room and down a passage, making them all keep very close to the bottom of the wall. It was a very good thing he did too, because round the corner they heard the sound of tremendous footsteps that shook the floor and made it tremble – the giant coming along the passage!

In a trice Mr Spells pulled them all into what appeared to be some kind of mouse-hole – it seemed as large as a cave to the children! They crouched there till the thundering footsteps had gone by. Then out they went as fast as they could.

'I want to find the front door if I can,' said Mr Spells. 'We can easily slip under that. It must be at the end of this passage.'

But before they reached it a thunderous noise made them all jump nearly out of their skins.

BANG-BANG-THUD-RAT-TAT-TAT!

'What is it?' cried Mollie, and caught hold of Mr Spells. 'What can it be?'

Mr. Spells laughed. 'I think I can guess what it is,' he said. 'It's Binky's cousin, Sleep-Alone. He's got tired of waiting for the castle, and he's knocking at the door to see what's happened! Oh dear – now I don't know *what* will happen!'

Plenty happened. When the knocker banged again on the door, an answering roar came from inside the castle, and Twisty the giant came pounding along the passage in a fine temper.

'Who's that knocking at my door? How dare you make this noise!'

The door was swung open and a wind blew down the passage at once, almost blowing the five tiny people over. Sleep-Alone stood outside, a small figure compared with the giant, but seeming like a giant now to the tiny children!

'Quick!' said Mr Spells, 'they are going to have a quarrel. Now's our chance to escape out of the door – but keep away from their feet. We're so small that neither of them will notice us.'

The children ran with Binky and Winks out of the door, keeping well to the side. But they couldn't possibly go any further than the top step because the drop down to the second step seemed like a cliff to them!

'I'll have to take a chance now and change us back to our right size,' said Mr Spells. 'Otherwise we'll have to stand on this top step and sooner or later be trampled on. Shut your eyes, please, take hands, and keep together. I haven't got time to draw chalk circles, so this spell will happen very quickly. As soon as you're the right size, run down the steps as quickly as ever you can, and go to that tree over there. I'll bring the Wishing-Chair, and we'll soon be off and away!'

'What about Sleep-Alone?' said Binky. 'We promised he could have the castle.'

'He'll look after that all right,' said Mr Spells, with a laugh. 'Sleep-Alone is bolder than I thought he was! Now – eyes shut, please, and hold hands hard.'

They all obeyed. Mr Spells said the words that undid the Go-Small Spell, and allowed them to shoot up to their right size again – but, as he had said, it happened very suddenly indeed, and all five of them gasped, felt giddy and fell over.

'Quick – get up – he's seen us!' shouted Mr Spells. He picked up the Wishing-Chair which had also gone back to its right size, and ran down the steps with it. Everyone followed.

Sleep-Alone and the giant had been having a real rough and tumble. The giant was stronger and bigger than Sleep-Alone – but Binky's cousin had got in so many sly jabs and punches that the giant had completely lost his temper.

He lashed out at Sleep-Alone, who ducked – but the blow just caught him on the top of his head. He stumbled – and that would have been the end of him if the giant hadn't, at that very moment, caught sight of the five prisoners tearing down his steps!

He was so tremendously astonished that he forgot all about Sleep-Alone and simply stood there, staring out of his saucer-like eyes!

Then, with a bellow, he was after them. 'How did you escape?' he roared. 'Come back – or I'll throw you all up to the moon!'

Mr Spells put down the Wishing-Chair. He sat in it quickly and pulled Peter and Mollie on his knee. Winks and Binky sat on the back. 'Home, Chair,' ordered Mr Spells, and at once the obedient Wishing-Chair rose into the air.

The giant made a grab at it, but the chair dodged, and Mr Spells hit the giant smartly on his outstretched hand. The giant yelped.

'Goodbye!' called Binky, waving his hand.

Meanwhile what had happened to Sleep-Alone? Plenty! When he saw the giant rushing after the others, he stood and stared for a moment. Then he grinned. Then he hopped into Wandering Castle and shut the door very quietly.

And when Twisty turned round to go back and finish his quarrel with Sleep-Alone, there was no castle there! It had gone on its wanderings again!

'Oh dear – I wish we could stay and see the giant looking for his castle,' said Mollie. 'What a shock he's having! His prisoners all escaping, the Wishing-Chair gone – and his castle wandering away in the forest with Sleep-Alone in charge. Won't your cousin be thrilled to have such a fine place to sleep in, Binky?'

The Wishing-Chair didn't go back to the playroom – it went to Mrs Spells' room.

They went in to see Mrs Spells, and told her their extraordinary adventures. To their surprise, Cinders was there and produced some excellent fruit buns that Mrs. Spells said he had just made. He really was a most remarkable cat.

Mollie glanced out of the window that looked out on the sea. 'Oh, look! she cried, 'there's our ship! *The Mollie!* I wondered what would happen to her. She's come back, Mr Spells.'

'Cinders brought her back,' said Mrs Spells. 'He knew the ship wouldn't be needed again.'

'It was a grand adventure,' said Mollie. 'I was scared at times, you know – but somehow I knew everything would be all right with Mr Spells there. Thank you, Mr Spells, for being such a good friend.'

'Delighted,' said the enchanter. 'Now it's time you went home.'

The children went to find the Wishing-Chair, which was still in the back yard. They climbed into it with Winks and Binky.

'Take us home, Chair!' cried Peter – and up into the air it rose, flapping its big wings – and in five minutes' time they were all back in the playroom once more.

CHAPTER 22

WINKS AND BINKY ARE SILLY

The Wishing-Chair seemed tired with all its adventures. It stood in its place for ten whole days and didn't grow its wings.

'We've only got a week and two days left before we go back to school,' said Mollie, who was a bit worried. 'I do hope we have another adventure before we have to say goodbye to you, Binky. Where's Winks?'

'I don't know. He was here last night, looking very mysterious,' said Binky. 'You know, the way he looks when he's up to some kind of mischief. I just hope he won't get into trouble.'

'You know he lost my doll's gloves on the last adventure? He says he dropped them into the sea,' said Mollie. 'Now his hands show up again – that awful blue colour!'

'I know. The things he loses!' said Binky. 'He came in without his shoes the other day, and said he'd lost them. I said: "Well, where did you take them off, Winks?" And he said he'd lost them without even taking them off. How could anyone do that?'

'Sh! Here he is!' said Mollie. 'Oh, *Winks!* Your hands aren't blue any more! They're the right colour! How did you manage that?'

'Aha-ha-ha!' said Winks. 'I've got a secret.'

'What is it?' asked Binky at once.

'Well, it won't be a secret if I tell it,' said Winks annoyingly.

'Have you been to see Mr Spells?' said Mollie.

'No. I went to see Witch Wendle,' said Winks. 'I borrowed her wand – it's got very good magic in it.'

'Do you mean to say old Witch Wendle lent you her wand?' said Binky disbelievingly. 'Why, it was only last week you told me you put her chimney pot upside down so that her smoke blew down into her kitchen. I don't believe you!'

'All right, then – but here's the wand, see?' said Winks, and he suddenly produced the wand from under his coat. It was a small, neat wand, not long and slender like Binky's. He waved it about.

Mollie and Peter stared in surprise – and Binky jumped up in alarm.

'WINKS! You took it without asking? I know you did. Witch Wendle would never lend her wand to you – why, look, it's absolutely *full* of magic!'

So it was. All wands glitter and shine and gleam and shimmer when they are full of magic, and this one was quite dazzling.

'I just borrowed it for a little while,' said Winks. 'The witch has gone to call on her sister. She won't miss it. I'll take it back soon. I wished my hands the right colour again – wasn't I pleased when they came all right!'

'You're a very bad, naughty brownie,' said Binky. 'You ought to go back to Mister Grim's school. I've a good mind to make you go back!'

'Don't you talk like that to me, or I shall lose my temper,' said Winks, crossly, and he poked the wand at Binky.

'Stop it,' said Binky. 'You should never poke people with wands. Surely you know that? And let me tell you this – I shall talk to you how I like. You take that wand back to Witch Wendle AT ONCE!'

'I don't like you, Binky,' said Winks, looking suddenly cross. 'I shall wish for a Maggle-mig to chase you!'

He waved his wand in the air – and goodness gracious, whatever was this extraordinary creature running in at the door?

It was rather like a small giraffe, but it had feathers, and it wore shoes on its four feet. It galloped round the room after Binky. The children fled to a cupboard. If this was a Maggle-mig, they didn't like it! Winks sat down on the sofa and roared with laughter. Binky was furious.

He rushed to the toy cupboard and felt about for his wand. He waved it in the air. 'Maggle-mig, change to a Snickeroo and chase Winks!' he cried. And at once the little giraffe-like creature changed to a thing like a small crocodile with horns. It ran at Winks, who leapt off the sofa in a hurry.

Winks waved his wand at the Snickeroo and it ran into the fireplace and completely vanished. Winks pointed the wand at Binky.

'Horrid Binky! Grow a long nose!'

And poor Binky did! It was so long that he almost fell over it! Winks took hold of it and pulled it.

Binky hit out at Winks with his own wand. 'Grow a tail!' he yelled.

And, hey presto! Winks grew a tail – one like a cow's,

with a tuft at the end. It swung to and fro, and Winks looked down at it in alarm. He tried to run away from the swinging tail, but you can't leave a tail that's growing on you, of course, and the tail followed him, swinging to and fro.

'Ha, ha!' said Binky. 'A brownie with a tail!'

Winks was crying now. He picked up his wand, which he had dropped. He and Binky hit out at each other at the same moment.

'I'll change you into a puff of smoke!' shouted Winks.

'I'll change you into a horrid smell!' cried Binky.

And then they both disappeared! Mollie and Peter stared in the utmost dismay. A little puff of green smoke blew across the room and disappeared out of the door. A horrid smell drifted about the room for a few minutes and then that went too.

Mollie burst into tears. 'Now look what's happened!' she sobbed. 'We've lost both Binky and Winks.'

Peter saw that the two wands were on the floor. He picked up Binky's and put it into the toy cupboard. Then he picked up the one Winks had taken from Witch Wendle's and looked at it. Mollie gave a cry.

'Don't meddle with it, Peter. Don't!'

'I'm not going to,' said Peter. 'I'm just wondering what to do about all this. It's very serious. I think we ought to take this wand back to Witch Wendle.'

'Oh, let's take it back quickly then,' said Mollie. 'And perhaps if we do she'll tell us what to do about Binky and Winks. How shall we find the way?'

'We might ask Mr. Spells,' began Peter, and then

suddenly stopped in delight. He pointed behind Mollie.

She turned and saw that the Wishing-Chair was growing its wings again! The buds on its four legs burst into feathers, and soon the big green and yellow wings were waving gently in the air.

'Oh! *What* a bit of luck!' cried Mollie. 'Now we can get in the Wishing-Chair and just tell it to go to Witch Wendle's!'

Peter sat in the chair and pulled Mollie down beside him. He had the witch's wand in his hand.

'Wishing-Chair, we want to go to Witch Wendle's,' he said. 'Go at once!'

The chair rose into the air, and made for the door. Out it went and up into the cloudy sky. It made for an opening in the clouds and shot through it. Now the children were in the sunshine above.

They flew for a long way, and then Mollie shouted in surprise, and pointed. 'Look! What's that? It's a castle in the clouds!'

Both children stared. It was a very surprising sight indeed. A big purple cloud loomed ahead, thick and gloomy. Set in its depths was what looked exactly like a castle, with towers and turrets. The chair flew straight to the cloud and stopped. It hovered just above the cloud, and the children couldn't get down.

'Go lower, Chair!' cried Peter. But the chair didn't. A head popped out of a window of the castle.

'Wait! I'll get you cloud-shoes! If you walk on the cloud without them you'll fall.'

The head disappeared. Then out of the castle came Witch Wendle, a bright star glinting at the top of her pointed hat.

She carried what looked like snowshoes, big flat things, to fasten to their feet.

'Here you are!' she said. 'Put these on your feet and you will be able to walk easily on the clouds. That's why your Wishing-Chair wouldn't land – it knew it would be dangerous for you without cloud-shoes.'

'Oh, thank you,' said Mollie. She liked Witch Wendle very much, because her face smiled and her eyes twinkled. The children put on the cloud-shoes and then stepped down on the cloud. Ah, they could get along quite well now – it felt rather as if they were sliding on very, very soft snow.

'What a strange home you have, set high in the clouds,' said Peter.

'Oh, people often build these,' said the witch. 'Have you never heard of people building castles in the air? Well, this is one of them. They don't last very long, but they are very comfortable. I've had this one about two months now.'

She led the way to her curious castle. 'We've come to bring you your wand,' said Peter. 'I must tell you all that happened.'

So he did, and the witch listened in silence. 'That tiresome Winks!' she said. 'He should never have left Mister Grim's school.'

'What can we do about Binky and Winks,' said Mollie, 'now that they are a puff of smoke and a horrid smell? Where have they gone?'

'To the Land of Spells,' said the witch. 'We'll have to get your Wishing-Chair to go there – come along!

CHAPTER 23

WHAT HAPPENED IN THE LAND OF SPELLS

The witch led the way to where the Wishing-Chair stood waiting patiently on the edge of the cloud, its wings flapping gently.

'That's a really wonderful chair of yours,' she said. 'I only wish I had one like it!'

They all sat in it. 'To the Land of Spells!' the witch commanded, and the chair at once rose into the air. It left the cloud and the curious castle built in the air, and flew steadily to the north.

'I'm very glad to have back my wand,' said Witch Wendle. 'Luckily it is only my third best one. If it had been my best one, the magic would have been so powerful that it would have shrivelled Winks up as soon as he touched it.'

Mollie and Peter at once made up their minds that they would never, never touch any wand belonging to a witch or wizard. Goodness – what a blessing that it had been the witch's third best wand and not her best one!

The chair flew on for a long while and the witch pointed out the interesting places they passed – the Village of Stupids, the Country of No-Goods, the Land of

Try-Again, and all kinds of places the children had never heard of before. They stared down at them in interest.

'What's the Land of Spells like?' asked Mollie.

'It's a strange land, really,' said the witch. 'All kinds of spells wander about, and bump into you – Invisible Spells to make you invisible, Tall Spells to make you tall, Laughter Spells to make you laugh – they've only got to touch you to affect you at once.'

'Oh dear,' said Mollie in alarm. 'I don't like the sound of that at all.'

'You needn't worry,' said Witch Wendle. 'They only affect you whilst they bump into you – as soon as they drift away you're all right again. We shall have to look for a puff of smoke and detect a horrid smell – then we shall know we've got Winks and Binky and I must do my best to put them right for you.'

The chair flew rapidly downwards, and landed in a very peculiar place. It was full of a blue-green mist and odd sounds went on all the time – sounds of rumbling, sounds of music, of bells, and of the wind blowing strongly.

They got off the chair. 'Now take hands,' said the witch. 'And keep together, please. You're all right so long as you're with me, because I am a mistress of all spells – but don't slip away for goodness' sake, or you may get changed into a white butterfly or a blue beetle, and I would find it difficult to know you again.'

Mollie and Peter held hands very hard indeed, and Mollie took the witch's hand too. And then all kinds of extraordinary things began to happen.

A little trail of yellow bubbles bumped into Mollie

– and, to Peter's great alarm, Mollie's neck grew alarmingly long, and shot up almost as tall as a tree! She was very alarmed too.

'It's all right,' said Witch Wendle. 'It will pass as soon as the trail of bubbles goes.'

She was right. When the bubbles flew off in another direction. Mollie's neck came down to its right size! 'You did look strange, Mollie,' said Peter. 'Don't do *that* again!'

It was odd to think of spells wandering about like this. Mollie began to look out for them and try to dodge them. She dodged a silvery mist, but it wound itself round Witch Wendle – and she at once disappeared completely.

'Where's she gone?' cried Peter in fright.

'I've still got hold of her hand,' said Mollie. 'I think she's only invisible – but she's here all right.'

'Yes, I'm here,' said the witch's voice. As soon as the silvery mist cleared away she became visible again and smiled down at the children. 'I didn't see that spell coming or I would have dodged it,' she said. 'Oh dear – here's an annoying one coming!'

Something that looked like a little shower of white snowflakes came dropping down on them. The witch changed into a big white bear, Peter changed into a white goat and Mollie into a white cat! That lasted about two minutes, and they were all very glad when they were back to their right shapes again.

They went wandering through the peculiar misty land, listening to the odd noises around, trying to dodge the spells that came near them. The witch put out her hand and captured a tiny little spell floating through the air. It looked like a small white daisy.

'I've always wanted that spell,' she said to the children. 'It's a good spell – if you put it under a baby's pillow it makes a child grow up as pretty as a flower.'

Suddenly Peter stopped and sniffed. 'Pooh! What a smell of bad fish!' he said. 'I'm sure that must be Winks. Can you smell a horrid smell, Witch Wendle?'

'I should think I *can*,' said the witch. She took a small bottle out of her pocket and uncorked it.

> 'Come here to me, you bad little smell,
> Into this bottle you'll fit very well!'

she sang. And the children saw a very faint purplish streak streaming into the bottle. The witch corked it up.

'Well, we've got Winks all right,' she said. 'Now for Binky. Look – here comes a puff of green smoke. Would that be him?'

'Yes!' said Peter. 'I'm sure it is. He and Winks would be certain to keep together.'

The witch took a small pair of bellows from under her long, flowing cloak and held them out to the puff of green smoke, which was hovering near. She opened the bellows and drew in the puff of smoke! She hung the bellows on her belt again.

'And now we've got Binky,' she said. 'Good! We'd better get back home now, and see what we can do with them. It's so easy to change people into bad smells and green smoke – any beginner can do that – but it takes a powerful witch or wizard to change them back to their own shapes again.'

They walked back to find the Wishing-Chair, still bumping into curious spells every now and again. Mollie walked into a Too-Big Spell and immediately towered over the witch and Peter. But she went back to her own size almost at once.

The witch bumped into a train of bright bubbles that burst as they touched her. When they looked at her they saw that she had changed into a beautiful young girl, and they were amazed. But she was soon her old self again.

'That was a nice spell,' she said with a sigh. 'I should like to have caught that spell and kept it. Ah, is that the Wishing-Chair?'

'Yes – but there's only half of it!' said Mollie, in surprise. 'Oh, I see – it's just been touched by an invisible spell – it's coming all right again now.'

Soon they were sitting in the chair. 'To the children's playroom,' commanded the witch. 'And hurry! The puff of smoke in the bellows is trying to get out. We'll lose Binky for ever if he puffs himself out, and gets lost on the wind.'

'Oh dear!' said Mollie. 'Do hurry, Wishing-Chair!'

The Wishing-Chair hurried so much that the witch lost her hat in the wind and the chair had to go back for it. But at last they were flying down to the playroom, and in at the door. Thank goodness!

The witch got carefully out of the chair. She took the bellows from her waist. 'Is there a suit of Binky's anywhere?' she asked. Mollie got Binky's second-best one from the cupboard. 'Hold it up,' said the witch. 'That's right. Now watch!'

Mollie held up the little suit. The witch took the bellows and blew with them. Green smoke came from them and filled the little suit, billowing it out, and – would you believe it? – it was Binky himself filling it out, growing arms and legs and head – and there he was standing before them in his second-best suit, looking rather scared after his curious stay in the Land of Spells!

Then it was Winks' turn. The witch asked for the teapot and took off the lid. She uncorked the bottle in which she had put the bad smell, and emptied it into the teapot. She put on the lid.

Then she lifted up the teapot and poured something out of the spout, singing as she did so:

> 'Teapot, teapot, pour for me
> A brownie naughty as can be,
> He's not as clever as he thinks,
> That wicked, wilful little Winks!'

And before the children's astonished eyes the teapot poured out Winks! He came out in a kind of stream, which somehow built itself up into Winks himself!

When Winks saw Witch Wendle he went very red and tried to hide behind the sofa. She pulled him out, saying, 'Who stole my wand? Who changed Binky into a puff of smoke?'

'Well, he changed me into a bad smell,' said Winks, beginning to sniff.

'He at least used his own wand to do it with,' said the witch. 'Winks, I'm sending you back to Mister Grim's school. You've a lot to learn.'

Winks howled so loudly that Mollie felt very sorry for him.

'Please,' she said, 'could he just stay with us till we go back to boarding school? We might have another adventure, a nice one.'

'Very well,' said Witch Wendle. 'One week more. Don't sniff like that, Winks. You bring all your trouble on yourself.'

'I'm sorry, Witch Wendle,' wailed Winks.

'You'll be sorry till next time – then you will do something tiresome once more and be sorry all over again,' said the witch. 'I know you, Winks! Well, goodbye, children. I'm very pleased to have met you – and, by the way, may I sometimes borrow that Wishing-Chair of yours when you are at school? It would be such a treat for me to do my shopping in it sometimes.'

'Oh, yes, please do,' said Mollie at once. 'It would be a nice return for all your help. You'll have to go to Binky's mother to borrow it when we're at school. He keeps it there.'

'Thank you,' said the witch, and off she went. Binky turned to Winks. 'We were silly to quarrel like that,' he said. 'I'm sorry I turned you into a bad smell, Winks. Go and wash. I still think you smell a bit horrid.'

So he did – and it was two or three days before he smelt like a brownie again. You just can't meddle with spells, you know!

CHAPTER 24
THE ISLAND OF SURPRISES

'You know,' said Mollie to Binky, 'we've only one more day before we go back to school. Mother has already sent off our trunks.'

'Oh dear,' said Binky, sadly. 'The holidays have simply flown! I do wish you didn't have to go to school.'

'Well – we love being at home – but we really do love school too,' said Peter. 'It's great fun, you know – and it's so nice being with scores of boys and girls who are our own age. I'm awfully glad we do go to boarding school, really, though, of course, I'm sorry to say goodbye to Mother and Daddy and you and the garden and Jane and the Wishing-Chair, and everything.'

'We never went to the Land of Goodness Knows Where,' said Mollie. 'I'd like to go before we leave for school.'

'Wishing-Chair, you *might* grow your wings quickly,' said Peter, looking at the chair standing quietly in its place. 'You really might!'

And, dear me, for once in a way the chair was most obliging and began to grow them! Unfortunately the children didn't notice that it was actually doing what it was told, and they went out into the garden to play.

The next thing that happened was the chair flying out of the door of the playroom, its wings flapping strongly! Luckily Binky caught sight of it, or goodness knows where it would have gone by itself. He felt the swish of the big wings, and looked up. The chair was just passing by his head!

He gave such a yell that Mollie and Peter jumped in fright. They turned, to see Binky making a tremendous leap into the air after the chair. He caught one leg and held on. 'Help! Help!' he yelled to the children. 'Come and help me, or the chair will go off with me like this.'

However, the chair went down to the ground, and allowed Binky to sit in it properly. Mollie and Peter ran up eagerly.

'Gracious! Whatever made us leave the playroom door open?' said Peter. 'The chair might have flown off anywhere and not come back. We shall really have to get a watch-dog for it.'

'It was lucky I just saw it,' said Binky. 'Well now – shall we go to the Land of Goodness Knows Where or not? Is there anywhere else you'd like to go?'

The children couldn't think of anywhere else, so the chair was told to go there. It flew off in the right direction at once. It was a lovely, clear day, with hardly any cloud at all. The children and Binky could see down below them very clearly indeed.

'Go lower, Chair,' said Binky. 'We'd like to see the places we're flying over.' The chair obediently flew down lower still, and then Binky gave a shout.

'Look – there's Winks! Isn't it Winks?'

It was. He too saw the chair and waved madly.

'Shall we take him with us?' said Binky.

'Well – it's his last chance of coming with us for a long time,' said Mollie. 'We said we'd let him come with us once more, didn't we, before he goes back to Mister Grim's school. We'll take him.'

So they ordered the chair to go down to the ground to fetch Winks. He was simply delighted. He clambered on to it at once. 'Did you come to fetch me?' he said. 'How nice of you.'

'Well, actually we weren't fetching you,' said Binky. 'The chair suddenly grew its wings, flew out into the garden, and I just managed to grab it in time. It was a bit of luck, catching sight of you like that. Winks, you must try and be good today – don't spoil our last adventure by being silly or naughty, please. We're going to the Land of Goodness Knows Where.'

'That's a silly land,' said Winks. 'Why don't you go somewhere more exciting – the Land of Birthdays or the Land of Treats, or the Village of Parties – somewhere like that.'

They were just passing over a big blue lake. They came to an island in the middle of it, and as they flew over it a surprising thing happened. Fireworks went off with a bang, and coloured stars burst and fell all round the chair. It was startled and wobbled dangerously, almost upsetting the children.

'Gracious!' said Mollie. 'What a surprise! What island is that?'

'Oh!' cried Binky, in great excitement, 'I do believe it's

the Island of Surprises! Isn't it, Winks? I really think it is.'

'Yes,' said Winks, peering down. 'It is! Look out, here comes another rocket or something. My word – what a lovely shower of coloured stars!'

'Can't we go to this island?' said Mollie. 'Binky, let's go.'

'Right,' said Binky. 'Mind you, the surprises may not all be nice ones – but if you're willing to risk that, we'll go.'

'Of course we'll go!' said Winks. 'Chair, go down to the island at once, please.'

Down went the chair, dodging another rocket. It landed on a patch of green grass, which at once changed into a sheet of water! The chair almost sank, but just managed to get itself out in time, and flew to a little paved courtyard.

'First surprise,' said Binky, with a grin. 'We shall have to be careful here, you know. Winks, you mustn't be an idiot on this island – you'll get some unpleasant shocks if you are.'

'Can we leave the chair here?' said Mollie doubtfully. 'It would be a horrid surprise if we found it gone when we came back for it.'

The chair creaked and flew towards Mollie. 'It says it's not going to leave us!' said Binky, with a grin. 'Very wise of it. Right, Chair, you follow us like a dog, and we'll all be very pleased.'

So the chair followed them closely.

The first really nice surprise came when they saw a table set out in the sunshine, with empty dishes and plates in a row. The children, Binky and Winks stopped to look at them. 'Is there going to be a party or something?' said Peter.

A small goblin came up and sat himself down on the form by the table. He stared earnestly at the plate and dish in front of him. And, hey presto, on the dish came a large chocolate pudding, and on his plate came a big ice-cream to match. He began to eat, beaming all over his ugly little face.

'Oooh,' said Winks at once, and sat down at the table. So did the others. They all stared hard at their dishes and plates.

Mollie got a pile of sausages on her dish and some fried onions on her plate. Peter got a big trifle on his dish and a jug of cream on his plate. Binky got strawberries on his dish and found his plate swimming in sugar and cream to go with them.

They looked to see what Winks had got. That bad little brownie, of course, had been tricky as usual. He had put *two* plates and *two* dishes in front of him!

But he wasn't looking at all pleased! On one dish had appeared a wonderful-looking pie – but when he cut the crust there was nothing in the pie. On the other dish had appeared a chocolate cake – and, as we know, that was the one cake that poor Winks simply couldn't bear to eat.

On one plate had come some steaming cabbage and on the other two prunes. How the others laughed!

'A pie with nothing in it – a cake he hates – cabbage – and prunes! Oh, Winks, what a horrid surprise. It serves you right for being greedy!' cried Binky.

Winks was cross. He stood sulkily whilst the others

tucked into their exciting food. Mollie was sorry for him and offered him a sausage.

The next surprise was also a very nice one. They finished their meal and then suddenly heard the sound of loud music coming from round the corner. They hurried to see what it was.

It was a roundabout! There it stood, decorated with flags that waved in the wind, going round and round, the music playing gaily. How lovely!

'How much is it to go for a ride on this roundabout,' asked Binky, feeling in his pocket.

'Oh, nothing!' said the pixie in charge of it. 'It's just a nice surprise for you. Get on when it stops.'

When the roundabout stopped, the children saw that there were all kinds of animals and birds to ride, and each of them went up and down as well as round and round. The brownies, goblins and pixies who had had their turns got off, and the children, Binky and Winks looked to see which animal or bird they would choose to ride.

'I'll have this pony,' said Mollie, who loved horses and always wanted one of her own. She climbed on to a dear little black pony.

'I'll have this camel,' said Peter. 'It's got two humps, and I'll ride between them!'

Binky chose a snow-white gull with outstretched wings that flapped as the roundabout went round. Winks chose a big goldfish. Its fins and tail moved in a very life-like manner. Winks cut himself a little stick from the hedge nearby. 'Just to make my fish swim well on the roundabout,' he said to the others as he climbed on.

'No whipping allowed!' shouted the pixie in charge. 'Hey, you – no whipping allowed!'

The roundabout started off again. The music blared gaily, the animals, fish and birds went round and round, up and down, flapping their wings and fins, nodding their heads and waving tails – all very exciting indeed.

And Winks was disobedient – he whipped his goldfish with his stick! 'Gee up!' he cried.

Then he got such a shock. The goldfish suddenly shot right off the roundabout through the air and disappeared! The roundabout slowed down and came to a stop. The pixie in charge looked very angry.

'He whipped his goldfish and I told him not to. Now I've lost the goldfish, and my master will be very angry with me.'

'Oh *dear*!' said Mollie, getting off her pony. 'I'm so very sorry. Winks did promise to be good. Where has he gone, do you think?'

Then there suddenly came the sound of a terrific splash, and a loud wail came on the air. 'That's Winks,' cried Peter, beginning to run. 'Whatever has happened to him?'

CHAPTER 25

HOME AGAIN - AND GOODBYE!

The yells went on and on and on. 'Help me! I'm drowning! Help, help, HELP!'

The children and Binky tore round the corner. The sea lay in front of them, blue and calm. The goldfish was swimming about in it, looking enormous. Winks was splashing and struggling in the water, and every time he tried to wade out, the goldfish bumped him with his nose and sent him under.

There was a crowd of little people yelling with laughter. Peter waded in and pulled Winks out. The goldfish flapped out too, and lay on the beach. It didn't seem to mind leaving the water at all – but then, as Mollie said, it wasn't a *real*, *live* fish. It was just a roundabout one.

'Winks, we're not a bit sorry for you,' said Peter. 'As usual, you brought your trouble on yourself. Now, just pick up that fish and take it back to the roundabout.'

The fish was big but not heavy. Winks groaned and put it on his shoulder. It flapped its fins and made itself as difficult to carry as it possibly could. Winks staggered back to the roundabout with it.

But the roundabout was gone. It had completely disappeared.

'Well,' said Winks, dumping the fish on the ground at once. 'I'm not carrying this fish any longer, then.'

But the others made him. 'We might meet the pixie in charge of the roundabout,' said Peter. 'And you could give it him back then. He was very upset at losing it.'

So Winks had to stagger along carrying the goldfish. Still, as Peter said, if he was going to make trouble, he could jolly well carry his own troubles!

It certainly was an Island of Surprises. There was a surprise round almost every corner! For one thing, there was a wonderful Balloon Tree. It had buds that blew up into balloons. Under the tree sat a brownie with a ball of string. You could choose your own balloon, pick it off the tree, and then get the neck tied with string by the brownie. They all chose balloons at once.

Winks stayed behind and they had to go back and fetch him. He had done a very surprising thing. He had picked six of the biggest balloons and had got enough string from the brownie to tie each of them to the big goldfish. And just as Binky and the children reached the Balloon Tree again they saw Winks set the goldfish free in the wind – and the breeze took hold of the balloons and carried goldfish and all high up in the air.

'Oh, Winks!' said Mollie. 'Now look what you've done!'

Winks grinned. 'Just a little surprise for the goldfish,' he said. 'Thank goodness I've got rid of him.'

Well, what can you do with a brownie like that? The others gave him up in despair and walked on again. The Wishing-Chair followed them closely, as if it was a bit afraid of the Island of Surprises.

Round the next corner was another surprise. There were a dozen small motor cars that seemed to go by magic. 'Come and race, come and race!' chanted a little goblin. 'The winner can choose his own prize!'

The prizes were as exciting as the little cars. There was a purse that always had money in it no matter how many times you took it out.

There was a little clock that didn't strike the hour, but called them out in a dear little voice. 'It is now twelve o'clock!' And there was a teapot that would pour out any drink you liked to mention.

'Ooooh – do let's try a race!' cried Winks, and he leapt into a fine blue car. 'I want one of those prizes!'

They all chose cars. The goblin set them in a row and showed them how to work them. 'Just press hard on these buttons, first with one foot and then with the other,' he said. 'Now – are you ready – one, two, three, GO!'

And off they went. Winks bumped into Binky and both cars fell over. Mollie's foot slipped off one button and her car stopped for a moment or two. But Peter shot ahead and won the race, whilst all the little folk cheered and clapped.

'Choose your prize,' said the goblin. Peter chose a little dish with a lid. It was a wonderful dish. Every time you lifted the lid there was some titbit there – a sausage or a bar of chocolate or an orange, or an ice-cream – something like that. Peter thought it would be very useful indeed to keep in the playroom.

They had a wonderful time that day. Once the surprise was not very nice. They went to sit down for a rest on some dear little rocking chairs. The chairs at once began to rock as soon as everyone was sitting in them – and they rocked so violently that everyone was thrown roughly out on the ground.

The goblin in charge laughed till the tears ran down his cheeks. 'Not a very pleasant surprise,' said Mollie, picking herself up and running after her balloon, which was blowing away. 'Funny to watch, I dare say – but not funny to do!'

They kept having titbits out of the Titbit Dish, but Mollie wished there were more ice-creams. So it was a lovely surprise when they came to a big public fountain, which had a tap labelled: 'Ice-cream Tap. TURN AND SAY WHAT KIND.'

Mollie turned it at once. 'Chocolate ice-cream,' she said, and out came a stream of chocolate cream that ran into a small cornet underneath and froze at once.

'Oh, look!' cried Peter. They had come to the little field, and in it were big white swans waiting to take people for flights in the air.

'Shall we have a fly?' said Peter. 'Do you think the Wishing-Chair will be jealous if we do?'

'I think one of us had better stay down on the ground with the chair, whilst the others are having a turn at flying on the birds,' said Mollie. 'Just in *case* it flies off in a huff, you know.'

So Mollie sat in the Wishing-Chair whilst the others chose swans and rose up in the air on the backs of the beautiful white birds.

When it was Winks' turn to sit in the Wishing-Chair

and stay with it, whilst the others rode on the swans, he thought he would get the chair to chase the swans and make them fly faster!

And up went the Wishing-Chair into the air and began to chase the swans, bumping into their tails and creaking at them in a most alarming manner. One swan was so startled that it turned almost upside down trying to get away from the Wishing-Chair – and the rider on its back fell headlong to the ground.

It was a witch! Fortunately she had her broomstick with her and she managed to get on that as she fell.

She was so angry with Winks! She called the Wishing-Chair to the ground at once and scolded Winks so hard that he tried to hide under the chair in a fright. Mollie, Peter and Binky flew down at once, angry, too, because of his mischievous trick.

'Ha, Binky!' said the angry witch, 'is this brownie a friend of yours? Who is he?'

'He's Winks,' said Binky.

'What – Winks, who turned his grandmother's pigs blue?' cried the witch. 'I thought he was at Mister Grim's school. Well – it's time he was back there. Swan, come here!'

A big white swan flew down to her. The witch picked up Winks as if he were a feather and sat him firmly down on the swan's back.

'Now,' she said to the swan, 'take Winks to Mister Grim's school and deliver him to Mister Grim himself.'

'Oh, no, oh, no!' wailed Winks. 'Mollie, Peter, don't let me go.'

'You'll have to, Winks,' said Mollie. 'You really are too naughty for anything. Try to be good this term, and perhaps you'll be allowed to spend your next holidays with Binky and us. Goodbye.'

'But I shan't get enough to eat! I always have to go without my dinner!' wailed Winks.

Peter couldn't help feeling sorry for him. 'Here – take the Titbit Dish,' he said, and pushed it into Winks' hands. 'You'll always have something nice to eat, then.'

Winks' tears dried up at once. He beamed. 'Oh, *thank you*, Peter – how wonderful! Now I don't mind going back a bit! I'll be as good as anything. I'll see you all next holidays. Goodbye!'

And off he went on the swan, back to Mister Grim's

school for brownies, hugging the Titbit Dish in joy.

'He's very, very naughty, and I can't help thinking that Mister Grim's school is the only place for him,' said Mollie. 'But I do like him very much, all the same.'

'Look, the sun's going down,' said Binky suddenly. 'We must go. They say the Island of Surprises always disappears at sunset, and we don't want to disappear with it. Quick – it's disappearing already!'

So it was! Parts of it began to look misty and dream-like. The children and Binky went to the Wishing-Chair at once. 'Home, Wishing-Chair,' said Mollie. 'Quick, before we all disappear with the Island. That witch has vanished already!'

And home to the playroom they went. They heard Mother ringing the bell for bedtime just as they arrived.

'Oh dear – our very last adventure these holidays, I'm afraid,' said Mollie. 'Binky, you'll take the chair to your mother's won't you, and take great care of it for us? You know the date we come back home from school. Be here in time to welcome us!'

'We'll slip in and say a last goodbye before we leave for school,' promised Peter. 'Don't be lonely without us, Binky, will you? And couldn't you go and see Winks once or twice at school – in the Wishing-Chair – just to cheer him up?'

'I'll see if my mother will let me,' said Binky. 'She doesn't like Winks, you know. Anyway, he will be quite happy with the Titbit Dish, Peter. It *was* nice of you to give it to him.'

'Goodbye, Wishing-Chair,' said Mollie, patting it.

'You've taken us on some wonderful adventures this time. Be ready to take us again next holidays, won't you?'

The chair creaked loudly, as if it too were saying goodbye. The bedtime bell rang again, this time quite impatiently.

'We must go!' said Mollie, and she gave Binky a hug. 'We *are* lucky to have you and a Wishing-Chair, we really are! Goodbye!'

Goodbye, too, Mollie, Peter, Binky, Winks and the Wishing-Chair. We'll see you all again some day, we hope!

More Wishing-Chair Stories

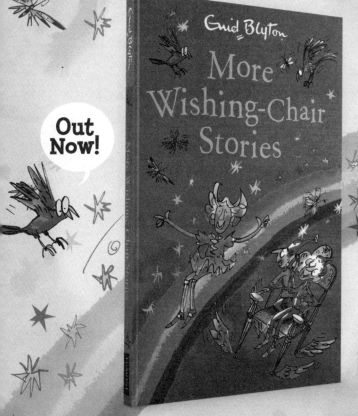

Out Now!

Join Mollie and Peter on the final magical
Wishing-Chair adventure from Enid Blyton!

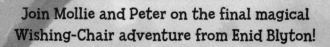

Available now in all good bookshops and online

Enid Blyton

*'Up the Faraway Tree,
Joe, Beth and me!'*

Joe, Beth and Frannie move to the country and find
an Enchanted Wood right on their doorstep! And in
the wood stands the magic Faraway Tree where the
Saucepan Man, Moon-Face and Silky the fairy live.

Together they visit the strange lands which lie at the
top of the tree. They have the most exciting adventures
– and plenty of narrow escapes!

Enid Blyton

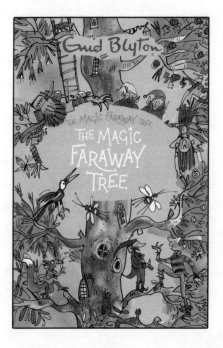

*'Oh, do let's take our lunch up into the
Land of Topsy-Turvy. Oh, do, do!'*

Rick thought it would be dull in the country with Joe,
Beth and Frannie. But that was before he found the
magic Faraway Tree!

They only have to climb through the cloud at
the top of the huge, magical tree to be in the Land
of Spells, or the Land of Topsy-Turvy, or even the Land
of Do-As-You-Please!

Enid Blyton

is one of the most popular children's authors of all time. There is an Enid Blyton book sold in the UK every minute. Her books have been translated into other languages more often than any other writer.

Enid Blyton absolutely loved writing for children. She wrote over 700 books and thousands of short stories. *The Famous Five* books, now 75 years old, are her most popular. She is also the author of other favourites including *The Secret Seven*, *The Magic Faraway Tree*, *Malory Towers* and *Noddy*.

Born in London in 1897, Enid lived much of her life in Buckinghamshire and adored dogs, gardening and the countryside. She was very knowledgeable about trees, flowers, birds and animals.

Dorset – where some of the Famous Five's adventures are set – was a favourite place of hers too.

Enid Blyton's stories are read and loved by millions of children (and grown-ups) all over the world.